THE
TYPESCRIPT
by
Jason Trench

Dales Large Print Books
Long Preston, North Yorkshire,
England.

British Library Cataloguing in Publication Data.

Trench, Jason
  The typescript.

A catalogue record for this book is
available from the British Library

ISBN 1-85389-770-1 pbk

First published in Great Britain by Doubleday, a division of
Bantam Doubleday Dell Publishing Group, Inc., 1988

Copyright © 1988 by Jason Trench

The moral right of the author has been asserted

Published in Large Print 1997 by arrangement with Robert
Harvey

Dales Large Print is an imprint of
Library Magna Books Ltd.
Printed and bound in Great Britain by
T.J. International Ltd., Cornwall, PL28 8RW.

THE TYPESCRIPT

Publisher William Dawnay has received an unsolicited manuscript written from the point of view of his late wife, and detailing events that led to her death in the Middle East twenty-two years previously. Dawnay, then a diplomat, and his wife Jill, were posted to al-Dawah but the claustrophobic outpost and the growing resentment of the natives soon began to tell on the couple. William grew disenchanted with Jill—but was he responsible for her death at the hands of a militant Islamic mob? His friends at the time thought so—and so does the person who has sent him the typescript...

FOR JANE

ONE

You lied to them. We had always slept together until that night. And I know why you lied.

Dawnay's self-control was such that he managed to lower the cup into the saucer, but his fingers involuntarily clung to the handle so that it toppled over half-full and the brown lukewarm coffee slurped sideways in a crawling puddle across the desktop, staining two letters, then advancing towards the tidy pile of unsuspecting manuscripts. Still he paid no attention: His gaze was fixed on the words of the professionally typed page, perfectly double-spaced without a single correction.

Sophie came in. 'William!' she chided. He drew himself up with a start: he was too distant a boss to be addressed by his secretary in that tone, although he didn't really mind. But she had lost her usual coolness when she saw the mess on the desk—and saw him do nothing about it.

'Oh dear. Did I do that?' he said with even more detachment than usual. She couldn't even begin to work out what made a dry old stick like him tick. She had worked for him for more than a year. He was an easy-going boss, if a little fastidious, so she stuck with him. He was kind too, in a remote sort of way. But his sense of humour was as bleak as a windswept moor; all sense of fun seemed extinguished from that pale, drawn, long face, those calculating eyes, that meticulous, overly precise way in which he entered the office, sat down at his desk, annotated manuscripts, dictated the occasional letter. Sophie had always assumed he was gay because he expressed so little interest in her; she had never been short of people—particularly older men—expressing such interest.

To him she was just another secretary, one of many who had passed before his desk; any thought of sex had long since been extinguished in him: They were there just to do their job. She was looking at him strangely and his hand moved imperceptibly to cover up the first page—the one with the sentence. 'Are you feeling all right?' she asked with genuine concern. Now that she asked it, he wasn't. He was feeling even worse than usual. He was sweating and felt strangely tired and weak throughout his body, which was odd because he hadn't had a taxing day. His eyes ached and it seemed to him that his heart was beating louder than usual.

'Not brilliant. I must have picked up a flu bug. They seem to be going the rounds.' He allowed a flicker of a smile to touch his face as he watched her briskly mop up the mess in front of him. Suddenly he felt an urge to escape her tough, young, uncomprehending efficiency, the orderly desk, the cluttered small room with its glistening table laid out with the publishing house's latest editions—good sellers all of them, geared to a commercial market, lacking in the elegance or discretion of the bygone era he still hankered after. He wanted to flee the book-lined walls, the view across to the next building. He had to read on, and he knew he could not do so here. 'I've got a doctor's appointment anyway. Won't do him any harm if I'm early. He always keeps me waiting when other patients turn up early,' he said, lifting the edge of his lips.

'Oh dear. I hope it isn't anything serious.'

'Stomach trouble. That's probably the cause of it all.' Inwardly he cursed the lapse. The news would be all round the building by five o'clock. And he was sure Sophie was having it off with Graham Bolton, the ebullient sales director. God, how he hated offices and their petty affairs and their politics.

He slipped the typescript into his briefcase and felt better in the cool air outside. The day was pleasant, with the sun attempting to seep through a thin white cloud cover. He wasn't going to his doctor, yet. He made his way along short streets overlooked by grey nineteenth-century buildings interspersed with greyer twentieth-century ones. They had been built to fit in with the surroundings, but they still stuck out a mile. From the world of scurrying office workers in dull suits, he came out upon Pall Mall's world of jean-clad, slovenly tourists. Dawnay found their slovenliness offensive and hated the denim uniform; but secretly he envied them the freedom to dress as they liked, and relished what jeans made of the better figures.

He didn't have much time for such

thoughts now. He strode up the stately steps of his club clutching his briefcase; he pushed through the swinging doors, not bothering to acknowledge the 'good afternoon, sir' that wafted across from the glass and mahogany booth that housed the porter. He ignored the stares from the stately portraits of forgotten diplomats that bedecked the club hall. An elderly member looked up, startled. Dawnay was a regular, and a slow, orderly and precious man; not one given to hurrying anywhere. The old man watched Dawnay disappear into the reading room before resuming the back number of the *Illustrated London News* he was reading.

Dawnay carefully surveyed the scene. The place was empty, except for four bores. One, in his late seventies, was asleep at the far end. Another, the club queen, who was eightyish, was ogling the first one; Dawnay reckoned he presented no danger. Of the two others, one was deep in the *Times*, and hadn't noticed Dawnay's entry. The last was a middle-aged antiquarian bookseller who regarded club membership as a licence to talk to any other member, irrespective of whether or not he had been introduced. His eyes had lit up as Dawnay appeared; it couldn't be helped. Dawnay placed himself by the window overlooking St James's Park, as far away from the active bore as possible, dangerously near, even, to the dormant one.

Dawnay felt reassured by his surroundings: the old clock ticking away; the long room; the worn brown leather chairs which dwarfed their inmates; the frail tables; the long windows overlooking greenery and the promise of a youth that had forever passed by the tottering old men in the room. A young black waiter was summoned to provide the odd port: he was an intrusion from the new life outside that the old men hated, yet one they were dependent on. He was somehow neutralised by his ridiculous tails.

Dawnay allowed himself two minutes before daring to open the briefcase with a click that he feared might arouse the attention of the predatory bore. He took out the volume.

He inspected it with caution, as though it were alive. The binding was plain blue cardboard, held together with two large metal clips, the product of any one of a dozen secretarial agencies that specialised in literary endeavours: he wouldn't trace

12

it that way. He cursed himself for having fallen for the author's trick, and opening it himself. Then he thanked God he had: someone else might have understood that it was directed at him. Out of the twenty or so unsolicited manuscripts that Smiley and Tollemache received every day, he made it his habit never to read one until it had gone through the system. The system was freelance readers, mostly authors or English lecturers, who for a small fee would tell him whether the book was worth reading. If it was, one of his younger staff might read it. If he or she okayed it, another reader's opinion might be asked, or the work might go directly to Dawnay if the subject was one that aroused his interest.

His own reading these days was quick, but, he liked to think, sleekly professional: he would read the first chapter carefully, speed up over the middle, slow down towards the end. Together with the reader's synopsis, that gave him all he needed to make an assessment. On the rare occasions when he was taken with a book, the editorial board would have to consider the typescript. They wouldn't read it, of course (all except Curtis Joll, one of the older directors, who believed in traditional ways). They would glance at the synopsis, hear his view, and attempt to shoot it down on commercial grounds. He rarely took unsolicited manuscripts up to the board, however good they were, because he had his own reputation in the firm to protect: books he put forward were unassailable from a commercial standpoint. Ninety-five percent of the firm's output was commissioned. But all publishers felt they had a duty to that increasingly mythical beast: the unknown author.

He would have pushed the book straight into his out-pile. But he had fallen for the trick: the author's name—Jill Robertson—was the maiden name of his late wife. It had given him a start; at first he thought it was a joke in bad taste by someone on the staff. Then he decided that nobody—for everyone knew the circumstances in which she had died—would stoop to that level. If it was a staff joke, the perpetrator would be out, Dawnay resolved grimly. He had wondered idly if there could be another Jill Robertson, if by an astonishing coincidence...

The first line had shattered that hope. It was blackmail, pure and simple. And he hadn't the first idea what to do about it.

'Bit early in the day to see you here, old boy?' said a voice from beyond his reverie. 'Playing truant?' The portly, creakingly jovial figure of the hippopotamus-throated antiquarian loomed over him.

'No—no. Actually, I'm reading a manuscript. I'm behind on it. I thought I'd get more peace and quiet here than at the office.'

'Oh. Oh, I see.' The expression of concern changed to one of dignified indignation at being told to push off. Dawnay had little sympathy to spare. There was nothing for it now but to read beyond that first sentence.

There, I've given the game away right at the beginning. Isn't that original of me? Or you would say naive and stupid, because you never had much respect for my mind. Nor for anything else, come to that, except for my face and figure—but don't let me start on that, or I won't say what I was going to say.

The same sudden rush of inconsequential thoughts. The same barely structured way of expressing herself. And she was right, of course, that he had never had much

15

respect for her type of mind.

He pinched himself. 'She didn't write this,' he muttered under his breath, 'it's a fraud.' He knew it was a fraud because she had never been self-critical enough to understand the contempt with which he viewed her, to the day of her death. Anyway, she was dead. How could it be anything but a cheap joke—or a blackmailer's expensive one?

'Can I get you anything, sir? Don't mind me saying, you don't look too good.'

He looked up angrily at the waiter's furrowed forehead. 'You could say the same, I daresay, of anyone who ever comes into this room. But yes. A brandy and water, please.' The sweat had glued his palms to the side of the leather chair, so that they came away with a crackle.

New paragraph. Start again. Try and be more collected and rational this time, because in argument it's reason that convinces, not emotion. It's what you say, not the force with which you say it. You taught me that, didn't you Will?

There I go again. I suppose I'd better begin with our arrival in al-Dawah. I won't forget that day. It was the day of the brightest hope that I think I ever had in my life—because everything afterwards was one slow downwards trudge. I'm exaggerating. There were moments of hope. But at that stage I thought life could not be improved upon.

Do you remember how naive and young and happy we were, Willie? I was twenty-three, you twenty-seven. Married only the year before. You were just that little bit wiser, more experienced than me—and I looked up to your worldliness, I thought it would help us in life. Even though I lacked your maturity it didn't mean that you were going to make all the decisions in our life together. We had met at a party, just a boring drinks party, full of empty people: and somehow, remember, we fell to talking to each other because neither of us had anything to say to the others there, although they seemed to have a great deal of nothing to say to each other. It's different for you now, isn't it? You enjoy the chatter now, of course. Or perhaps you feel you must pretend to do so.

Anyway. It's strange how two people who think they know each other after a few meetings because one conversation takes place between them don't really know each other at all. I thought you liked me for my thoughtfulness. I never thought of myself as

17

beautiful, so it never entered my head that that was what attracted you; too many people have told me since that I am for me to doubt that that is what has most impact on those I meet.

I was attracted by your looks too: the long, thin, thoughtful face, the slightly untidy dark hair, as though you didn't care too much about outside appearances. The slightly sardonic eyebrows and the turn of the mouth—which showed you had a sense of humour although then I didn't realise what a hard, bitter, razor edge it had. Do you remember the dinners we had in the months of our engagement? They were the most joyful evenings of my life, I hung on your every word; and you weren't playing to an audience so you were tolerable.

No, I'm being bitchy. I loved you, and you were adorable then. The parents were a bit of a strain, but we gritted our teeth bravely and fought through. My parents hated yours: they resented your parents' 'Let's-get-the-whole-thing-over-as-quickly-as-possible' attitude intensely. A mere doctor's daughter; my father's attitude was that at least he had tried to help people, while your father had tried only to get rich. I don't mind telling you that now, although I'm sure you guessed at the time. Never mind; it was worth it to live happily ever after. God, though, the wedding was an ordeal! All those relations that I had never seen before and was never to see again!

And the honeymoon—in Paris, of all clichéd places. It was a bit of a joke. Remember how just to be conventionally unconventional we'd gone to bed together for the first time a fortnight before the wedding. I made you think it was the very first time for me: it wasn't—three years before I'd had an affair with a solicitor twenty-two years older than me. But you were too polite—or inhibited—to ask why there was no stain on the sheets. Do I shock you, Willie? Girls think like that, whatever they are taught to say to men. It certainly wasn't your first time: you were practiced, and if I wasn't so nervous, I would have complimented the way you tried to make it pleasant for me.

Paris would have been all right, if we hadn't had to do so many things, like inspect the Louvre day after day from top to bottom until we had seen every minor statue and Impressionist and visited every church and café in the city. And then there were the addresses your parents gave you, and all those boring old people that felt they had to entertain us while we had to be polite... I know, at the time I didn't complain, but that was because I was walking on air.

And then three months later your brilliant career brought you your first posting abroad to al-Dawah. I couldn't imagine anything more idyllic, more romantic than to be a diplomat's wife in some remote, faraway, dangerous Arabian country—me, for whom Paris was my first trip abroad! I can remember every detail of our arrival, the scrub desert all around the aircraft as far as the eye could see—or at any rate to the ridge of low hills; being met by Colonel Pugh on the tarmac, and being wafted through the special VIP door for diplomats—remember the looks the other passengers gave us! And into the Land Rover, with its own driver, which hurtled along the narrow tarmac road, hooting at the lorries as we overtook whole queues of them—rackety contraptions barely visible in their own dust. There was so much to see, to wonder at, you couldn't take it all in: the wagons with their mules and camels, all heavily laden with baskets and packing cases; the ragged shack houses along the bottom of the hills; the curious structures on the tops. The deep blue sky, so strong in colour it looked like a painting.

Can you remember the Taj, where we spent the first two weeks while we were looking for a flat? I know a hotel room isn't a home, but I enjoyed it. And that extraordinary bar—the only one in the city—outside the embassy circuit that is, because alcohol was frowned upon—under the fake nomadic tent inside the hotel lounge? Where beers cost three pounds each and those furtive little men turned to stare because no woman had ever crossed the threshold of such a place before? The whole hotel was so absurd: built in the Indian grand style, all marble and pillars, in the middle of the dirtiest, poorest, yet most sophisticated city in the Middle East.

Do you remember the day after we arrived, being taken to the embassy by the colonel? How kind he was, full of good humour and jokes about the place that we couldn't quite understand?

I'm going to put you into the third person now, because this is a book, and I have submitted it to a publisher, and it makes it easier for me to detach myself from the subject. You—I mean Willie—were beastly when we got out and the colonel parked the car in the diplomatic enclave behind the hotel, in a leafy suburb of secluded villas with well-watered gardens. 'The colonel's quite a character, isn't he? Small moustache, hail-fellow-well-met manner, plummy voice, red face—he's almost a stage Englishman.'

'He seems very kind,' I said, reprovingly.

'He's either been touched by the sun or he's come to play the part that's expected of him so well that it's taken over his personality.'

'I'm looking forward to meeting his wife.'

'I just hope we don't go the same way.'

The embassy forecourt was a pleasant little yard, behind a high white wall, with a little desiccated lawn in the middle. An ornamental basin of earth squatted in the middle. In the heat, it seemed unlikely anything would grow in it. There was a little triangle of steps leading up to the embassy's main door; the building itself was Western-style, built a century before by a well-off merchant. It was orderly, in a European way, low-key, only three stories high.

The ambassador himself came out to greet us. He was a rather squat and burly man, with a large battered smile that colonised the southern half of his face, forcing his eyes into slits and even his forehead into creases. He was barrel-shaped, wearing an old-fashioned double-breasted white suit, with the jacket unbuttoned. He beamed as we came up the steps. Willie was in his best suit, although he had a white one: it was a lightweight dark grey. Thank goodness I was a little more appropriately clad in a plain white blouse and a discreetly ornamental skirt.

'How d'you do, sir?' Will said formally.

'Delighted to have you here, delighted to have you. Good of you to come and join us,' said the ambassador expansively, shaking hands first with me and then with Willie. As if Willie had had any choice. 'I think you'll find the place interesting, although it's a little quiet at the moment—just the civil war as usual in the south and a few tribal rebellions in the north.' He chuckled, a nautical, mirthful sound. Willie gave him his mirthless grin in return, and I smiled.

It was a relief to get out of the sun into the cool of the dark hall. The ambassador noticed. 'I daresay you're finding it hot—of course, it's only your second day. This is deep winter. Just wait until spring, never mind summer.' He chuckled again. 'I've arranged a little drink, dear boy—I hope you don't mind me springing this on you—with your colleagues of the next few years. It's a small family, as I'm sure you know. Her Majesty's government in its wisdom doesn't attach too high a priority to this posting, and—' he said, clearing his throat—'it must be admitted that trade with Britain is not as large as might be desirable. But I think you'll find yourself very much at home.'

He wafted us into the embassy dining room. There were only six people present. The ambassador made the introductions. 'My wife, Edwina. David Pugh, of course you know. Mrs Pugh. Peter Quennell, the commercial attaché, and Mrs Quennell. Hugo Hennessy, the minister, my number two. You'll get to know them very well, I'm sure.' They all smiled back; we whirled round, talking to them all. They were intensely curious: Had we had a previous posting, when were we married, they were sure we'd settle down splendidly, was there anything we needed—they'd be delighted to help out.

'It seems a wonderful little set,' I said late that evening as I combed my hair in front of a rather exotic dressing table with five mirrors on it, provided by the hotel. 'And the most fascinating country!'

'We're going to get bored out of our tiny minds,' said Willie tersely from the shower.

'I think that's a little unfair. We hardly know them.'

'They're so few. And they're all incestuous. And they're all caricatures. I thought the colonel was bad enough. But his wife's a catty old trout if ever I saw one. The ambassador's like the Captain in Moby Dick—all jolliness, no substance. His wife's a *grande dame*—for an embassy of six people. Quennell and his wife are a couple of provincials. Hennessy's the only one with any personality at all.'

'I think you're very hasty to judge these people so quickly,' I said feelingly.

'Nonsense. First impressions are always right,' he replied cheerfully. I slammed the door of the bathroom, to let him know what I felt. It was the first time we had really disagreed.

Willie settled into his office easily enough. It was spacious and reasonably cool when the fan had been on for a while. The secretary, a cheerful Scottish girl, said it was 'absolute hell' in the summer.

Willie seemed almost disheartened by how light his work-load was. There were some routine duties, like going through the newspaper in the morning (Willie was an accomplished Arabic speaker), reporting on the political articles. Otherwise it was largely up to him. Once a week he wrote a despatch, culled from the press, about the political situation; this the ambassador as often as not sent on, with only a few words changed (usually for grammatical reasons) as his own despatch. When the ambassador wanted someone else to attend meetings with low-level political officials, which was usually all the embassy got to see, Willie saw to them; those of greater importance were met by H.E, as everyone called him. Arrangements to suit the occasional visiting journalist or adventurous M.P were made by Willie, although the ambassador saw to their social side. But the visits were few and far between.

An awful lot of the work, for me, was the socialising that went on between embassies. Willie revelled in it. I was much more interested in finding out about the country I was in. I was fascinated by its architecture, its customs, its religion, its people.

It was I who pressed upon Will that we should live in the old city. Al-Dawah was split into two by the River Ibb, a wide, sluggish, oil-smooth slick that wended its way south, providing the main source of irrigation in a country where only the slopes of the mountains were otherwise fertile. The embassy quarter, and the modern part of the city, were on the west bank. The east bank was the site of the old city which was surrounded by a dried-out old gully where there could never have been enough water to make a moat of; and the poorer slum quarters, miserable hardboard-and-tin dwellings mixed in with tents of indescribable filth in which these semi-nomadic people kept their children and animals.

The old city could hardly have been more of a contrast to the embassy quarter. The overcrowding and the lack of modern streets, lighting or sanitation were the same as in the new city. Dirt tracks ran between the houses and filth-caked gutters on the sides of these; sewage was merely thrown from pails out of the windows, although the place smelt less than you might expect.

But from the moment I saw it, it seemed almost unearthly beautiful. It was such a relief; on the stop-over at Riyadh in Saudi Arabia I had seen no trace of an old city: just a large, half-finished building site of hideous modern blocks, hotels, and broad avenues. Even at al-Dawah the modern part of the city was tatty, run-down and dusty, with purpose-built blocks which were slowly falling apart. The roads were pot-holed and the pavements broken. There was nothing Arabic, or even distinctive, about it—although the embassy quarter had some lovely merchants' houses. But the old city was proof that the twentieth century had spared something in the Arab world—and that what had been spared had infinitely greater worth than anything that could be built today.

The old city consisted mainly of the earliest form of skyscraper. There were large *palazzi*, almost Italian-style, built one floor on top of the other, added to perpendicularly, vertiginously, as a family got richer. The method of building looked decidedly unsafe—many of the buildings were crazily tilted, or looked top-heavy; but they were all rather elegant, displaying a curious architectural grace that was heightened by the elaborate decoration on the exterior. The windows varied according to floor and position. There were little round windows, like port-holes, on some floors, particularly the upper ones. There were fine, stately windows, some with glass, some without, of astonishingly perfect perpendicular proportion to the building, as though imposed by an English architect on the controlled disorder of the city. These were usually surrounded by magnificent white crenellated ornamentation. There were more modern, narrow, slit windows, usually without glass, of a medieval style. All the rows of windows were placed carefully and decoratively, with regard to the overall look of the building; the little carved window ledges were similarly ornate. The buildings were partly coloured by the brown mud bricks of which they were made: but they were also painted, floor by floor, layer by layer, with a magnificent whitewash that was sometimes merely a decorative band, sometimes a massive artistic flourish, covering the side of a whole floor with elaborate motifs.

The overall effect was the most extra-ordinary jumble of harmonious, often lopsided, tall, decorated, embossed buildings which in some cases looked statelier than Venetian palaces; in others their white decorations made them look like crazy, delicious chocolate cakes. Add to this the narrow patchwork of alleys that criss-crossed between the buildings, so that it was easy to get hopelessly, happily lost wandering through them; and the children in rags who played wildly and cheerily down the alleys; and the scuffling, angular, dark-skinned men in black jackets that detracted from the tunics they wore down to their sandals; and the women in their spectacularly beautiful shawls—embossed greens and blues mainly—and the occasional goatherd leading his sheep between the buildings. All of it transported me into another age. It was like living in one of those old prints of Rome or London before the advent of the road, the motor car and the electric light.

I was first taken to the old city by Mrs Quennell, the commercial attaché's wife. She was a brisk, no-nonsense middle-aged woman, who advised me to wear a hat—both against the sun and because Arab men thought that any woman who did not cover her hair had loose morals—and a long skirt as well as a white blouse. She made a reassuring companion and would ignore the hard gaze of the men at the sight of these pale-skinned women on their own in a strange capital. We walked blissfully about. She could see I was in a trance: 'I know. That's what I felt when I first saw it.'

She showed me the soukh, where men sat on their haunches and bargained away, looking furiously at one another, barking and snarling their way through the buying process, leaping to their feet and stalking off only to be called back to a lower price and a fresh tot of bitter black coffee: business was conducted seriously in al-Dawah.

We didn't penetrate the heart of the soukh, where the shed-like stalls were clustered together as far as the eye could see, because we were too much an object of hostile curiosity to them. This was male territory; they would put up with forwardness in foreigners, but not in a male preserve. 'I've never seen local women here,' said Mrs Quennell, whom I was soon calling Lavinia. I peered, fascinated, into the wooden stalls where they sold what I judged to be the national symbol of the country—curved daggers, usually in black-and-white wooden sheaths hanging from green-and-red embossed belts which bore inscriptions in bold black Arabic lettering. When I peered into one stall, the man glared angrily back: daggers, especially, were male with a capital M.

Mrs Quennell was a thoroughly practical, down-to-earth type who chatted incessantly. But I enjoyed her company. She was no effort to talk to because she did all the talking. And beneath the chatter she seemed to be genuinely interested in the place she was in. 'If you like this, you'll like the ruins of Qadar,' she said. 'They're northwest from here—near the Saudi border.'

'I'd love to go. Will you take me there?'

'I'd be glad to. The trouble is, the accommodation isn't all that wonderful. No Hotel Taj there.' She chuckled.

'You know what I'd like to do most of all,' I said mischievously. 'To live here, in the old city.'

She didn't bat an eyelid. 'Would you? I'm not sure I could put up with the scruffiness, or without having some seclusion, or a garden. Still Hugo does...'

'But there are gardens! Look there.' There was a huge, broad green square we had come upon from the quiet alley we had walked down, where the facade of the mini-skyscrapers was at its most stately—like a London square unexpectedly stumbled upon. The greenery, the shrubs, the palm trees were peaceful and exotic in their dry, dusty, mud-coloured surroundings.

She pointed out a tidy white dome and a small, twisting minaret beside it. 'It belongs to the mosque. Only the mosques have them. They always do. Don't ask me why.'

'Still—to have lived in al-Dawah and not to have lived in the old city! I'd always regret it afterwards,' I said with feeling.

'Hugo seems happy enough here. He lives in the wealthy part—beyond the end of the garden. The part that is connected up with electricity and sewers. Look, I'll show you. I don't doubt you'll be invited to dinner there in time.' There was something in the way she said it that told me she didn't much like him.

Hugo Hennessy had us to dinner, sure enough, just four evenings later. There were eight of us, including him. Pairing him was a good-looking, strong-boned woman of about forty, who turned out to be the cultural attaché at the American Embassy. She talked in a rather world-weary, non-stop drawl about art in New York. There was the French minister and his wife: he was thin and fastidious, with glittering eyes and a look of malign mischievousness. She was very unlike him, rather plump and jolly and looking as if she must have been very pretty thirty years before. They were in their late fifties; she drank like a fish. The Pughs and ourselves completed the party.

The American cultural attaché acted as hostess, a job she had clearly done before; but we were served by two discreet Arab houseboys, both in immaculate white, both very slim, very dark with good looks and rather graceful movements—different from the usual short, squat, surly inhabitants of al-Dawah, I thought. The silver and the plates were clearly not foreign office issue, I thought ruefully. Hugo was a man of private means.

He was a difficult man to describe. He was rather good-looking, in a conventional way, with a thin, distinguished, long face, a nose that was long and could only be described as aristocratic, and a thin-lipped but rather set mouth. He didn't have an ounce of spare flesh on his body, although his face had that slightly larger-than-life fleshiness endowed by years of good health and good living. His hair was spectacularly blond, neatly parted. He was very much the suave, gracious host. Together with his American companion's sophistication, there was something about him that made me nervous.

There was also something about him that kept him from being as attractive to women as he could have been—to me, at least. He was somehow too collected, too sure of himself. The smile was turned on at the appropriate time and place; there was no warmth in it. And I thought there was a good deal of malice in those shrewdly watching, laughing eyes. Also he was somehow too perfect, too impeccable. His face looked almost as though it had been made up. But he went out of his way to be nice to us at dinner, and my suspicion of him was almost dispelled by the time we stopped eating.

It was the house, though, that really interested me. To go in, you had to pass through the lower floor where the animals were kept. And so they were: two mules and two dogs, looked after by a ragged individual with a rather wild-eyed look, who didn't say anything as one of the two houseboys led us to the stairway. This ascended into a large, spacious lobby with a smooth tiled floor, in sharp contrast to the straw and filth in the menagerie below. This was the *piano nobile,* where the reception rooms were: The ceiling was high and the furniture rather dull, black and wooden; but the carpets and wall hangings helped to offset any effect of heaviness. The large windows indicated it was quite a light room during the day. I was enchanted. I immediately told Hugh that I wanted to live in the old city. He was surprisingly forthcoming.

'Do you really? I thought I was the only one with these exotic tastes!' he exclaimed. 'Well, as matter of fact I know that there's a flat, or two floors, up for rent in this building. My landlord was telling me about it only the other day. He lives in the same building, you know. I occupy this floor and the one above. He's got the two above that, an old widower lives on the one above that, and then the two above are free. There's a couple above that: the building is ten floors high altogether, you know. Rather remarkable how these chaps build without knowing a thing about prestressed concrete and the rest of it. If you're really interested, I can pop up and see him. I'm sure he'd let me have a key to show you after dinner.' I said I was, although Willie looked dubious, even a little embarrassed, that I had raised the matter.

At dinner I was placed beside Colonel Pugh, who didn't say a word to me throughout the evening, being entirely occupied with the American cultural attaché. The French minister beside her chatted away with Mrs Pugh on his other side, who also gave liberal helpings of her conversation to Willie. Hugo sat on my right, making easy conversation about the country and answering my questions, but giving the minister's wife, who was on his right, a fair amount of time.

Willie and the minister's wife appeared to get on like a house on fire. I realised for the first time that he was quite good at this sort of thing, and even enjoyed it, whereas I was bored. They were all too old for me, although I didn't mind Hugo. Still, I would come to enjoy it in time, I decided without enthusiasm. The trouble was I didn't know what to talk about, except to ask questions, while they all seemed to be very self-assured and were not much interested in my answers when they asked me questions. They talked chiefly about people in other embassies, whom we didn't know, and what they were up to, and about politics.

At the end of dinner the conversation became general. Hugo made it so deliberately, leaning forward and interrupting the minister in midflow. 'What makes you think Salim Haddad's day is past?' he asked sharply.

The Frenchman, sensing he had an audience, spoke louder, with theatrical gestures. 'Haddad represents the old politics, the old Middle East. He is a patron. He derives his power from the *haute bourgeoisie* and the merchant classes. He is being bypassed. A country like this needs younger men, dynamic men, who are not afraid to tread on toes. The Sultan knows that. He is no longer so young he can be manipulated by an old cynic like Salim.'

'You mean al-Ashraf?' asked Hugo casually.

The French minister made a dismissive gesture with the cigarette he had lit up over his cognac. 'Of course.'

'You don't think he's too lightweight?' asked the colonel gruffly.

The minister rounded on him. 'You should know, Colonel. What weight does a man need if he has the army behind him? He doesn't need to be intelligent. He can just install technicians, people who will do the job of modernising the country. What has Salim ever done? This place is falling apart—you only have to walk down the street to see that.' The Frenchman leaned forward. 'But let us hear your view. Do you think he has the army behind him?'

'Yes,' said the colonel bluntly. 'Al-Ashraf's a young man—hell of a young man to be army commander—thirty-eight. But here they respect youth: It means he's still got his wits about him. The younger officers regard him as one of them. The older generals were jealous when he was appointed, three years ago, but he's taken care not to give them offence.'

'He hasn't succeeded in putting down the insurgency—either of them,' Willie put in.

'Doesn't matter,' said the French minister, not cuttingly. 'The fact that the rebellions are growing in size makes the army all the more important to the country.

The Sultan entirely depends on the army now. And the soldiers are getting more and better equipment, which keeps them happy with al-Ashraf. Besides, they love fighting.'

'Would you gentlemen mind if we excused ourselves to powder our noses,' said the American cultural attaché, with a dazzling smile. They all laughed politely at the cliché, and we went off to talk among ourselves. The French minister's wife was friendly, asking how I liked the country, offering tips on living there. Mrs Pugh soon butted in to gossip about mutual friends, while I had a polite talk with the cultural attaché, which quickly petered out.

It was a relief when the men came in. Both Hugo and the French minister chatted with me, and Hugo later took us to see the upstairs apartment; everyone came to have a look. It was devoid of furniture, but the rooms were spacious, well-proportioned, and not too low: there was a recently installed kitchen and a Western-style bathroom. I visualised the drawing room with lighter, more modern furniture than Hugo had in his. It was my dream. 'The managing director of an American trading company lived here before,' said Hugo. 'He seemed quite happy with it. The windows are smaller than mine, but at this level they aren't overlooked by the house opposite.' We moved in two weeks later.

It was only three or four months after that that I began to notice the change in Willie. Perhaps there wasn't a change. Perhaps that's how he had always been, but I, in my romantic haze, had never noticed it. Or perhaps the change was in me, although I didn't think so. All I knew was that I didn't like it. It wasn't that we rowed, as most couples do a few months after their marriage, 'establishing their territorial rights,' as I think I once heard Colonel Pugh call it. It was the way in which I began to sense that Willie was distancing himself from me. Not in private—not yet anyway. But he began to interrupt me in conversation, as though to correct me, to say something more intelligent—or more like what he thought the person I was talking to wanted to hear. He seemed almost to patronise me, exchanging knowing smiles with the people I talked to, as though I couldn't be expected to know any better.

41

Oh, I know he had a much better understanding of the local politics, which bored me to tears, as the men talked of nothing else. But I was a different person. I didn't want to know about politics. He also got into the embassy gossip side of things with a swing, and I drew no pleasure at all from doing down other people. I wanted to talk about pleasant things, about the place, about ordinary life there, but even the people who enjoyed talking to me about such things seemed to bore Willie.

At the time I put it down to Hugo's influence: Willie and he seemed inseparable. I could see the admiration and respect in Willie for Hugo's style. In fact it was Hugo who persuaded Willie to drop his opposition to our living in the old town, as I wanted. I didn't mind Hugo that much: he was always polite, and even a little protective towards me.

But Willie also got on well with the Pughs. She was a ghastly, name-dropping, reputation-carving woman who would barely speak to me, so I didn't see why I should speak to her. And he was almost as bad. I had liked his Blimp style at first. But he was just as vicious as her when it came to laughing at other people.

I had no doubt that I was the butt of a lot of their jokes, even if Willie wasn't.

Instead I got on with the Quennells, and Willie couldn't stand them. Above this tiny world, the ambassador and his wife drifted on another plane; but I must say they were always friendly enough, and talkative enough on the innumerable social occasions when we met them.

The social occasions: There were the dinner parties, most of them just like Hugo's. There were the formal receptions at our embassy, which were mercifully shorter. There were the receptions at other embassies, which one went to out of a sense of duty. Always the same people, always the same conversation, although I soon found that some of the starchier-looking wives of opposite numbers were quite human—quite like me, I suppose that was the same thing!—to talk to.

There were the functions within our own embassy for the staff and the English community—what there was of it—five secretaries, one consul and about ten expatriates, all of whom belonged to an informal club which had the right to use the postage stamp of a swimming pool behind the ambassador's residence once a week, and to have tea in the garden there, or play badminton—the embassy didn't run to a tennis court. I enjoyed their company the most, although there were some intolerable ones who tried to ape Mrs Pugh. But I found the socialising interminably dreary when there was so much else to do.

The flat took up a lot of my time—furnishing it. Willie didn't have the time or inclination to interfere much, luckily; he just vetoed the things he absolutely hated. The difficulty was in finding furniture of any quality at all that wasn't that heavy, gloomy stuff pillaged from old colonial houses that seemed to be in vogue in al-Dawah. At length I thought I had furnished the flat reasonably respectably—in diplomatic good taste but with a teeny bit of life and colour to it, to show we had some character apart from that endowed by diplomatic life. As Willie said, there was a danger that the service would take us over: that we would become stereotypes. It was so easy to fall into the style of conversation of dress, of living which you had to observe so much of the time, all of the time. But I thought it was Willie who was in danger of falling, not me.

We had a flaming row about our first dinner party in our new flat. We felt we couldn't invite H.E.—although he had had us to dinner right at the start—not for the first one, not until we were more practiced at that art. Hugo, who had found us the flat, was invited of course. Willie decided to ask Ed McQuarry, the country's sole English journalist. How he managed to keep body and soul together on the few lines or so a month he got into the *Daily Telegraph* defeated me! But as he was both political and press officer combined, Willie felt responsible for him, and I think McQuarry had proved a mine of information for him. The rather severe lady director of the British council was chosen to partner him. Willie claimed he was a misogynist, and chuckled at the thought. The prettiest embassy secretary was invited to partner Hugo.

The trouble was that Willie wanted the Pughs, and I wanted the Quennells.

'It would just be a carbon copy of Hugo's party,' I said. 'Can't we try something different?'

'The Pughs make things go with a swing. They're amusing. You have to work so hard with the Quennells.'

'I don't find them difficult to talk to at all!'

'You wouldn't—' he said, and checked himself. 'Hugo can't stand them, you know that.'

'Why should Hugo decide who we have at our dinner parties?'

'He's not deciding, for God's sake! It's just we want the thing to be a success, don't we?'

'Yes, and I want to invite people I like, not people I can't stand.'

'What do you have against the Pughs? What have they done to us?'

'What haven't they done? Always gossiping, always being bitchy. They've never asked us...'

'That dinner at the Quennells was the most boring occasion I've ever attended in my life.'

'Instead, I enjoyed myself for once! Just because they weren't what you call amusing—putting other people down.'

'Jill, don't be such a bore and a prig.'

I was holding a glass of wine, which I could have flung in his face. Instead I just stalked out of the room and burst into tears. But he didn't come to make it up.

I cried myself to sleep, fully dressed. He

must have slept in the spare room. I didn't see him in the morning. When he came back from the office he behaved as though nothing had happened: He was his usual dry, sardonic, detached, but—underneath it—tender self. I had lost all urge to carry the argument on.

Just before we went to bed he said, 'All right, it's the Quennells. But promise me the Pughs get invited next time.' I promised, with a flood of kisses. But I had the impression he had surrendered just to get things on an even keel between us again, not because he felt he was in the wrong.

The dinner party passed off tolerably well. Hugo made an effort to be pleasant to the Quennells, who enjoyed themselves thoroughly. Peter Quennell was usually a rather grim, taciturn man; but he relaxed visibly and his good humour conveyed itself to Willie, who nevertheless spent most of the evening talking to Hugo across the tops of the heads of the two women.

The journalist, McQuarry, a small puffy-faced Scot with a somewhat seedy manner and a look of feigned incredulousness, was quiet most of the evening, seeking out other people's opinions, rarely venturing his own. It was his profession, I supposed. He chainsmoked and chaindrank his way through dinner, but I liked him. I felt sorry for him, a fifty-five-year-old bachelor for whom life had become this out-of-the-way place. Perhaps that was his secret weapon, how he got people to talk: They felt sorry for him. He cornered Hugo and had a long, earnest, quiet chat with him. We women enjoyed ourselves, moaning together that the men never saw fit to talk to us for long.

Even Willie had seemed in relatively good spirits afterwards. And yet the feeling that he was drifting away from me grew stronger over the next few weeks. We didn't have another row, but he came back later and later from work, and I knew there wasn't any special reason for it; he enjoyed work more than talking to me, that was all. Anyway, that's what I felt, although I tried to persuade myself otherwise. He didn't talk to me very much when he did get back. If there was a cocktail party, we would meet there and I would go on home afterwards alone, because he had work at the office to finish. He always used to pester me to make love, in the first weeks after our marriage; now he never did, and I was afraid to ask him in case he said no.

Sometimes he would arrive very late, and explain that he had been driven home by Hugo and asked to his flat for a drink. He was never angry or unpleasant just a little distant and cool, as though we were flatmates, not husband and wife. Over long weekends he relaxed sometimes and became the Willie I had known at the beginning of our marriage—only a year before—and we would talk and kiss and make love. But such occasions grew less frequent. What I most resented was the way he put a distance between himself and me when we were out socially, as though in some way he was taking the side of whoever was putting me under the social microscope. I threw the occasional tantrum when he behaved like that, but he said I was imagining it, and we would sleep apart—a bed had now been put in the spare room upstairs. There was never any point in continuing the quarrel next day.

Words on paper hardly describe how I began to feel. There had been so much hope in me, and there was so much to like about the place and so much that was exciting about our lives. And yet my mind was dominated by the fear that Willie no longer loved me, that he was beginning even to despise me.

And as the feeling grew, I resolved to do all in my power to make Willie love me. If he wanted me to get on with Hugo and the Pughs, I must get on with Hugo and the Pughs. If he wanted me to drop the Quennells—well, I wouldn't do that, I needed some real friends, but I would distance myself. He was the most important thing in my life. I must compromise, not fight him, if I wanted to be happy. The trouble is that I couldn't get on with the Pughs and many of the people Willie liked in other embassies because they didn't seem to want to talk to me.

One day at a Friday afternoon tea at the residence Lavinia said, 'You remember about the ruins at Qadar? The Queen of Sheba's capital. You said you would like to go. Why not during the bank holiday weekend?' I had no plausible excuse for not going, and I knew it would be regarded as a slight if I said no, and besides I wanted to see the ruins! I said yes. Willie glared at me when I told him I was going with

Lavinia; but otherwise he said nothing.

The weekend was the last long one before the summer would become too hot for us to go. Even so, when we set off in the comfortable air-conditioned Rover that Lavinia had badgered out of the ambassador (it was the embassy's number two car, after the faintly ludicrous Rolls that H.E cruised apologetically about in), we were only just comfortable.

On the trip across, we stopped for petrol. I got out to stretch my legs and the heat hit me hard, like a physical force, so that I was almost kicked back by it. After experiencing the furnace outside, it was marvellous to get back into the breezy car again. Lavinia had brought three thermos flasks of cold tea, coffee and water, and they were a blessed relief.

We spent the night in a hotel just 120 kilometres from the site. It was a hotel only in name. We had to share a room, there was an unbelievably filthy communal lavatory, and we ate our own food. Lavinia had brought netting to keep the hundreds of flies off us.

But luckily it was quite cool by night. We left before dawn because by about eleven-thirty it would be too hot to inspect the ruins. We arrived at seven-thirty and spent a dreamy three hours wandering about, exploring them in the strangeness of the barren range that marked the divide between al-Dawah and Saudi Arabia. The mountains were round-topped and low, like bald old men; and the ruined city itself was a suggestive network of walls, ditches, earthworks and pillars, extending for hundreds of yards.

As Lavinia, who knew all about the place, explained where the temple, and the villa of the queen, and the market square had been, I felt absorbed by the mysticism of this eerily empty place, so close to the site of one of the biggest deserts in the world, so far from habitation even on our side of the mountains. The driver took us back by a road that ran along the ridge of the mountains which was remarkably remote and evocative. There were few villages in the region, but many wadis and camping nomads.

'It was T.E. Lawrence who described how the cycle of Arabia worked,' said Lavinia. 'Al-Dawah was the fertile, pop-ulated part of the peninsula, with more people than the whole of the rest of Arabia put together—around seven million.

52

Too many, however, for the land to sustain. The surplus population was forced eastward, onto the mountains and the lower slopes—over there—to try and scratch out a living for their flocks on the sparse grasslands that were too arid for fixed settlement. So the people became nomads, trekking from oasis to oasis in the desert down below. Over a period of generations they went on a gradual movement to the north, to Iraq and Syria, where they would find fertile, underinhabited land and settle down again. It's like a great human whirlpool in the sand.' I listened fascinated, and not for the first time wondered at the erudition and imagination of this woman who, on first acquaintance, seemed the most practical kind of English suburban housewife.

We returned to al-Dawah after dark the next day. After all the fun and the merriment—the two of us had drunk two bottles of wine when we stopped for a picnic lunch inside the car (I had the impression Lavinia's husband was not someone she ever had that much fun with) I steeled myself, going up the stairs, for the indifferent welcome, the half-smile of greeting, the languid 'help yourself to a drink' I was beginning to know so well. Instead, when I let myself in, he was standing and looking at me from the sitting room with a strangely tender expression on his face. He came forward and held me and buried his face in my shoulders for what seemed like minutes. Then he kissed me hard: 'I missed you,' he said. I was too surprised and pleased to answer him.

As the houseboy, Sabah, prepared the dinner of chicken and rice and we drank stiff gin-and-tonics, the story came out.

'Hugo gave me a ring on Saturday. "As you're an abandoned husband this weekend, why not come down and have dinner with me?"' He did; they ate alone.

Hugo had been extraordinarily candid and expansive. 'You've been here for five months now. What do you think of the setup?' Willie had answered non-committally. 'I think it stinks,' said Hugo. 'The worse thing is we're served by an ambassador who couldn't tell a can of worms if it was set on a plate before him. He's an incompetent and phony stuffed shirt. Takes no interest in politics, just likes riding in that Rolls of his, performing ceremonial functions, promoting exports.

That's all they ever think about now, him and that chip-on-his-shoulder grammar-school boy, Quennell. I'd like to know how much Britain's exports to al-Dawah have increased since he came here!

'It's all the F.O's fault. After the war we had the new meritocracy in the service. Eton was out; Oxbridge was out. Chaps had to have brains. They were going to set the world to rights. Instead, because they were phony, they were far snobbier than we could ever be. The worst thing is they didn't have the experience or the upbringing to know what makes a man like Salim Haddad, from an old family, tick. I wonder how I managed to survive in the service, or how I stood it.' And so on he went in this vein. He had obviously had quite a lot to drink before Willie got there, and he drank a lot more through the meal and afterwards.

'They don't know what's going on,' Hugo said. 'But I can tell. That old fool Grantley thinks that the army's taking over, meaning lots of exports for British arms manufacturers. That Salim's being edged out. Certainly, that's how it looks on the surface. That tin soldier, al-Ashraf, is never far from the *infante's* side (Hugo always referred to the seventeen-year-old Sultan as the infante). But don't mistake appearances for reality. It was Salim who got al-Ashraf appointed in the first place as commander-in-chief. Why? Because he wanted someone who didn't have real standing in the army to run the army: someone without, in the dear old parliamentary expression, bottom. Salim has his men in the army who will push al-Ashraf aside if he ever gets too uppity. Al-Ashraf knows that: Don't you think he'd have had Salim dismissed as prime minister otherwise?

'As for the Sultan of course he resents Salim's power. But Salim has control of the middle classes, he knows how to handle the tribal chieftains, he's indispensable to the Sultan. Also the Boy Wonder doesn't want the army to push out Salim: He'd be the next to go. It's that wily old bird Salim Haddad we ought to be sucking up to, not that thug in tin.'

'What about the National Liberation Front guerrillas in the south?'

'The communists don't have a chance in a country like this. That's another thing the ambassador's mis-read, and no doubt you have.'

Hugo got up from his chair and sat

down beside Willie on the sofa. 'The rebellion, the fighting, has tied the army down in the south of the country. Al-Ashraf doesn't have the units in the capital to stage a coup; and the Sultan and Salim know it. The fighting weakens the army's influence in the capital, far from strengthening it.'

'At this stage,' Willie went on tensely, draining his glass with an odd expression and reddening, 'Hugo put his hand on my knee. Paternally, I thought. I didn't do anything: I asked him another question, I can't remember what. Then—then he made a homosexual advance.'

I looked incredulous. 'Good heavens. What did he do?'

'I'm not going to say,' said Willie. 'It's enough to say that it was a pretty crude one and left no doubt as to—ah—his intentions.'

I pealed with laughter. 'Oh Willie. I thought you had long realised he was queer. It's nothing to get so worried about.'

He glared angrily, 'I imagine you realised?'

'Isn't it obvious? He's so affected. And well turned out, and he's unmarried. Those manservants of his! Lavinia and I were

57

laughing about it only yesterday. Lavinia was so worried for you. I said you were most definitely not queer. I could give her my word for that. You could look after yourself.' I couldn't help my laughter.

'That's the sort of thing you talk about with that woman? And you consider the Pughs bitchy?'

'It's just so funny, that's all.'

He stalked off angrily, slamming the door. I laid back in a chair, still convulsed with laughter. I couldn't take it seriously. I really couldn't. I didn't even try to make it up to him that night. He was sullen and resentful for days afterwards, and still I couldn't bring myself to apologise. But he never went down to drink with Hugo alone again.

Dawnay put down the typescript carefully and looked about him, as though he feared that his reactions—the burning sensation that had come to his cheeks, the sweating, the slight trembling of his fingers—were being observed. Even at this distance—twenty-two years—the events of that time hurt; why shouldn't they? They had changed his life.

He had been reading so intently, he

hadn't noticed the room gradually filling up as the after-work crowd arrived. Outside, the windows were struck by the peculiar slanting intensity of the late evening sun. The new arrivals were mostly elderly men, civil servants and foreign office officials with parchment cheeks and shuffling gait; men he hardly knew, yet guessed were infinitely more powerful in their Whitehall empires than he, or the politicians who postured nightly on television screens.

They greeted each other with detached friendliness, tall bald men and small white-haired men, all in pinstripe or dark suits, their faces bearing expressions of a responsibility remote from those affected by their decisions, worn down by years of paperwork and departmental infighting. They were there for a quick drink or a quick read of the newspaper, or to meet someone for dinner, or to meet their wives before going to the theatre; these women would be herded into the single room near the entrance where women were allowed to assemble, like a race apart.

For Dawnay it was a relief to be able to get away from women. Besides, they didn't want to see the men shaking off the dust of their work, in all their seediness. The men

59

were all so old, so slow, the place suddenly seemed unbearably sad.

He realised he had welcomed the distraction from the—the book. Just by reading it, he hoped he would arrive at an answer about what to do. He assumed that it would turn out to be a cheap fraud, even a ghastly joke, something he could take to the police and go through a bit of unpleasantness which would soon be settled, or better still which he could throw away. But the novella was too damned penetratingly accurate, down to the last emotion, the last description. Whoever wrote it had been there!

Oh, there were mistakes, of course, the last the most glaring of all: Of course he had realised that Hennessy was queer, it had been perfectly obvious from the moment he met him. But it was one thing to be a latent homosexual and another for Hennessy to try and take advantage of him, as he had that night in the flat; again the flush of embarrassment. After that Dawnay had had to distance himself, of course.

Then there was Jill. She was beautifully portrayed: the half enthusiastic, half hesitant manner, like a child finding out just how much it can do. The inane prissiness and the hatred of anyone who was half amusing. The sense of superiority and self-sufficiency, which to everyone else looked like inferiority. God, how he hated her still: especially for what she had done to the rest of his life. Portrayed in those pages was the Jill he remembered: the same disinterest in social life, and the same fascination for local colour, like some nineteenth-century missionary's wife up the Zambezi. The same uncanny ability to read his mind, to discern his motives and what he thought of her. She couldn't have known as much as the book portrayed, surely; he had concealed his attitudes skilfully, he thought. She couldn't have had that much intuition—

He nearly pinched himself. This was a work of fiction! Not written by her, but someone putting thoughts into her long-dead mind. Someone who had known her, and him and the whole chain of events in al-Dawah that had led up to the tragedy; known them all too well. But it wasn't—couldn't be—her.

He saw that he hadn't touched the drink he had ordered earlier. He carefully put the manuscript into his briefcase, took a sip, and then leaned back in the leather chair, fingers stretched together in front of him as though meditating or praying. What was to be done? He had to be dispassionate, analytical; wasn't he famous for being so? Should he take no notice? The typed, unsigned covering note had simply stated that she—he, whoever—was sending it to him first, for possible publication. That suggested that she would try others: blackmail was implied. No, he couldn't sit back.

Should he go to the police? He would have to explain why it was blackmail, then. There wasn't the slightest chance, after all these years, that anyone would assume that there was a grain of truth in the accusation—there wasn't!—but word might get out. If the blackmailer were caught, he would presumably go on trial and the allegations would come out in open court, might get into the press. All the details of that ghastly affair would come out again. Dawnay considered the prospect with utter weariness. Couldn't they have left him in peace? And what did they want anyway? Money? He hadn't much to give. Revenge? Who could possibly hate him that much, when the only person with reason to do so was long dead? Malice? Ageing did strange things to some people.

He was groping his way towards the conclusion he knew he would have to reach in the end. He must find the blackmailer himself, without involving the police, without involving anyone. But where to begin? How to set about it? God, he'd read so many crime novels and none of them even began to approximate real life! Here he was, a stranded individual without the slightest idea of how to go about a piece of detective work. Of course, it must have been someone who was present at the time. But how to set about tracing them down, after so long...

It was too late to start tonight anyway. He'd be late for his appointment with the doctor. And for that tiresome dinner party Sarah had insisted on having. He finished his drink, and got up. His legs were curiously weak and wobbly. He felt somehow shrunken. He decided he would have another drink on the way out, in the little crush bar downstairs, to forget about the whole business and face up to the evening. He made his way through the room, exchanging a nod and wan smile with someone who recognised him. The small bar was empty, just the barman washing glasses and another member sipping a drink in the corner.

With a start, he caught the other man's eyes: they were wide for a moment. Dawnay supposed his own expression must have been that of a trapped rabbit. The same carefully groomed, sleekly polished appearance. The same pale blue eyes that appeared to have no spark behind them, but just watched. The same fine, chiselled features. The same careful, self-conscious poise.

Hennessy recovered first. 'My dear Willie: how splendid to see you. God—it must be more than twenty years!'

The bonhomie was professional, exaggerated, and caught Dawnay only momentarily off-balance. He recovered, to freeze his smile before it was half formed. He knew now who had written the book. The coincidence was too great. If the bastard had waited even a day—

'Hello Hugo. What brings you here,' Dawnay said coldly, shaking the proffered hand slightly, picking up his drink and making for a chair.

The man was nearly nine years his elder; he looked dismayed. The smile stayed in place, however. 'You haven't changed any,' he said quietly.

'You have—more than might be expected.' Dawnay examined with satisfaction the deep pouches under the eyes and the lines radiating out from the corners; the worry in the forehead, the sagging at the side of the jaws, the thinning of the shocking blond hair—now dyed, surely?

Hennessy's expression turned to puzzlement; his chin dipped into his collar. 'Yes, well it hits us all. You're lucky to have a few years in hand yet.' Hennessy suddenly looked straight at him. 'As a matter of fact, I'm not here by chance. I was hoping to bump into you. Rang your office: they told me I'd catch you here.'

'Yes, I know.'

'Rang you, did they? Well, can we have a word?' He motioned Dawnay to his table.

'I suppose I haven't got much choice,' said Dawnay dryly.

'Of course you have,' Hennessy said, with a trace of irritation. 'I know it's a long shot.' He suddenly glanced at Dawnay angrily. 'My, aren't you publishers grand chaps. Much grander than us diplomats.'

Dawnay was determined to keep his

advantage. 'Still in the service, then, after all these years?'

Hennessy laughed. 'Of course. I've got four years yet to retirement, you know.'

'I didn't mean that. Somehow I thought you'd be one of those who gets bored of it all. You were bored enough in al-Dawah—when you were still young.'

'Bored! You must be joking. Al-Dawah was the golden year. Most interesting place I've been to. Bloody revolution—' He caught himself. 'I'm sorry I forgot. I imagine it still hurts after all these years.'

'It does,' said Dawnay vehemently, lowering his glass and looking levelly at him. 'It does.'

'Yes, well,' said Hennessy, examining the bowl of peanuts in front of him. 'My next posting's Brazil. It could be my last, or there may be one more. I'm looking forward to it. It's hot, and the people are beautiful, and it's important. It's beginning to interest even those idiots down in King Charles Street. I could have done worse. The kids'll love it—'

'You're married?' asked Dawnay, surprised.

There wasn't a trace of embarrassment on Hennessy's side. It was as though he had forgotten his behaviour in al-Dawah and was genuinely a happily married man. 'Yes, of course. Three children. I heard you had remarried. Any children?'

'No,' said Dawnay tersely.

'Wise man,' said Hennessy, that avenue closed. It was he who broke the silence. 'Look, old boy, the reason I wanted to talk to you—'

'I know,' Dawnay said, and Hennessy looked startled. Dawnay felt a certain smugness about his powers of deduction. 'It's about the book, isn't it?'

'How did you guess? Who told you about it?'

'It's not very well written. I'd reject it in the normal course of things,' Dawnay said with a note of disdain.

Hennessy's face registered dismay. 'Really? But you haven't read it.'

Dawnay said slowly, 'Let's finish with all this—this preamble. And get to the point. After all, it's not much fun for me. What are you doing it for? Money? It can't be for money.'

Hennessy swallowed distinctly. 'No, I suppose not. I suppose it's a subject that's always gripped me, and one about which I have some knowledge. And I've always wanted to write a book. It's a fancy, a conceit, if you like. But I think it'll sell well enough,' he added hastily.

Dawnay looked at him in astonishment. 'I should hope not,' he said dryly.

Hennessy looked hard back. 'What are you talking about?'

'The book I received in the post this afternoon.'

Relief flooded into Hennessy's eyes. 'No, no, there must be a mistake. I haven't sent you the book yet. Thought I'd sound you out first, see if you were interested.'

Dawnay looked at him disbelievingly. 'Go on.'

Hennessy cleared his throat. 'When I was ambassador to Portugal, I came to know the British community out there rather well. There's a longstanding British tradition there, you know. I thought it might be interesting to do a book on the community. The port trade, for example, is absolutely fascinating. They've got their own club, the Port Wine Institute. It's more British than the British—'

But Dawnay wasn't listening. He was wondering. He was wondering whether he really could believe this was a coincidence: that this man was really wanting to sell him a book wholly unrelated to the slim volume that had dropped on his desk that afternoon. If not, what was his game? Surely, if he had written the book, he would have made at least a veiled reference to it, instead of prattling on about Portugal?

Hennessy could see Dawnay wasn't listening. He ended limply. 'Well, I just thought you might look at it.'

'Of course, of course.' Dawnay made an effort. 'It sounds fascinating. Why don't you send me a copy—if you haven't already.' He watched Hennessy closely. Not a flicker—just a slight gleam of hope.

'Not yet—but I'll put one in the post. I thought I'd better have a word with you first.'

'You've never felt the urge to write earlier in your career—for example, about the al-Dawah affair, which you witnessed pretty closely?'

Again, not a flicker. 'Yes—but somehow one was always doing other things. Remember how much there was to do on a posting. One always put off putting pen to paper. It's only as I've grown older that I've wanted to leave something behind. Somehow, although one has led a full life, nobody remembers most things about it now. Isn't it strange how one can sail through life without leaving a trace. Perhaps that's just something diplomats suffer from. I'm sure you did the right thing getting out.'

He still hadn't risen. Dawnay said, 'Don't go by me. I changed my job because I had to. I couldn't have gone on after what happened. I needed a complete break. I found one. Publishing's a bit of an ivory tower, in a way. One meets other civilised, pleasant people, and thinks the higher thoughts, and keeps away from the real world outside. And yet, in its own way. It's very competitive—something everyone wants to do. I've been happy enough with the life: more satisfied, I think, than I was with the ephemera of diplomacy. I can point to the books I've published.'

'But you didn't write them.'

'No, but the idea as often as not is mine: the commissioning, the execution of the project from start to finish. In diplomacy, you hoped that through negotiation, through persuasion, through chatting up someone's wife at a cocktail party you might be influencing him. But you could never be sure. I think I have had greater satisfaction in publishing.'

'My God, though, I wouldn't have missed some of the places I went to! Brunei, Zanzibar, al-Dawah itself.'

'You enjoyed that?'

He bridled. 'I'm sure I groused about it a bit at the time. But yes, I even liked our curious colleagues there—all except that damned Grantley. And he had his reasons for the attitudes he took. Never mind that; even that plump bourgeois businessman, Quennell, that talkative wife of his—I didn't mind them. And Colonel Pugh—remember that preposterous moustache and those flushed cheeks. Mrs Pugh was a live wire, though,' he added, with a sly look at Dawnay.

Dawnay parried. 'I still can't imagine you with a wife and children. Why did you get married?'

Hennessy drew himself up. 'I fell in love. You should know. You were married twice. Today—my children give me something extra, something I didn't have.'

'You believe in falling in love,' said Dawnay with a sceptical smile.

'Yes, don't you?' asked Hennessy, surprised. 'You certainly seemed to be in love with Jill—' he stopped, and then went on, 'at the time. I can't imagine you not being in love with your present wife—' But it was too late. He had betrayed himself by the look in his eyes. He had betrayed his suspicion.

And in that moment Dawnay knew he hadn't been responsible for the book; he would never have tried to cover up as clumsily as that if he had. Suddenly all his old weariness returned. He was beginning to hate himself for the life he had led; he blamed Hennessy for not sharing his half-existence, his living a life that was bearable but no more. Hennessy was an old bugger who hadn't deserved a good life. Dawnay wanted to shatter the complacency of this undeserving man who had achieved peace.

'You should enjoy Brazil. They say anything goes there.'

Hennessy's face, assumed a fixed expression. He glanced at the door, where a tall elegant woman in her mid-fifties with bony features, a taut smile and rather bright blue eyes had just come in. She looked a little like Hennessy himself. 'Darling, how did you persuade them to let you in here,' he exclaimed incredulously.

'They tried to stop me. I'd been waiting

twenty minutes in that beastly, boring family room.'

'Darling, this is Willie Dawnay, who was in the embassy in al-Dawah.' She smiled, and from her look Dawnay knew she knew all about him. 'Goodness, look at the time. Sorry, Willie, got to rush: the play starts in fifteen minutes.'

They left Dawnay with his drink, with his thoughts, and with the certainty that Hennessy was not the man. But if not, who was? And how to start searching?

There was a fine patter of rain as he walked the few steps from his car to their comfortable three-storey house in Whiteley Street, a cul-de-sac off the King's Road. The road was secluded, and well away from the endless parade of youthful fashions that amused or irritated him, depending on his mood. Tonight they would have irritated him. He would ring the doctor's office to say he could not make the appointment tonight, but would tomorrow. But he couldn't slide out of dinner.

Sarah was in a fluster when he arrived. 'Couldn't you have got home a little earlier. They'll be arriving any minute.'

'Sorry, darling,' he said, preferring to avoid a fight, as he usually did. 'Problems at work. Quite unexpected. I must have a bath.'

The doorbell rang. 'You can't. They're here.'

'You talk to them.'

'But I'm cooking!'

He slipped off upstairs anyway. She made a face, rearranged it and went to the door. It was Penny, his wife's unmarried sister. That was alright. She would be able to help in the kitchen. She was there to partner Dafydd Howard, one of Dawnay's most promising young writers, who was unmarried. The other guests were Alex Moylan, one of Dawnay's less successful writers, a bearded and extremely slow-talking man who had been at university with him, and whom he kept on the list for old times' sake; and his second wife—young, intense, good-looking and empty-headed. At best she would decorate the dinner table.

He adored Sarah, he mused as he dressed himself. At forty-two she was still extraordinarily good-looking, with a face that had only just begun to permit the odd wrinkle, and a luminescent skin

74

that was not too taut across her magnificent cheekbones. Her straight blonde hair was swept back in a long ponytail that cascaded down her back. This evening she was dressed informally, in rather strident pink trousers that curved appealingly inwards where they met her thighs, doing justice to the well-proportioned thighs and behind. A slightly embossed white shirt, open two buttons, revealed the imminent surge of her breasts. He thought of her long slender arms punctuated by the thin watchstrap as he combed his hair.

He slipped on a brown checked shirt without a tie, and comfortable trousers. He felt better for the bath. Downstairs he greeted his sister-in-law with the smile and tense kiss that passed for a warm welcome from him. She wasn't as good-looking as her sister, being too thin, but the fine bone structure was the same; tempting enough, he thought, even for a young man like Dafydd. Still he wasn't trying to match them up; he just hadn't been able to think of anyone else to ask.

The Moylans arrived; both were elaborately informal. He wore a carefully tied cravat, a red shirt, and designer corduroys. He looked very plump and self-satisfied behind the nonconcealing grey scrub of a beard. She was nervous and gushing as always. She was one of those women who could talk ceaselessly without saying anything, who could be equally friendly to everyone she met. Alex watched her with amused tolerance. It was obvious enough why he had married her; it certainly wasn't for her mind. Perhaps he just needed her to keep him awake.

Dafydd was last to arrive, as usual, and the only one to look as though he hadn't dressed for the party but always looked this way, which was more smartly informal than any of them. He was at least twenty-eight, maybe thirty, but he looked about twenty. His fair hair was cut very carefully, a flop forward at the front, just over his collar at the back. He had a boyish, mischievous look, and his face lapsed frequently into an easy, laid-back smile. He was wearing just a brown shirt, a thin blue pullover and ordinary jeans. Dawnay had taken to him the moment he had entered his office. His novel had been a conventional enough one, a semi-autobiographical first work about a youth disenchanted with life; but it had that sparkle of phrase, that unexpectedness in the way the words were put together, that told Dawnay that he had got a winner. His uncle had been a writer too, of rather readable biographies, which was how the boy had got an introduction and Dawnay to read his manuscript in the first place. The gift clearly ran in the family.

Dawnay refilled his glass and chatted with his guests; he tried to focus on their words, to chase the thought of the typescript from his mind. He had wanted these two to meet, although the dinner party had been Sarah's idea. She was rather fond, Dawnay suspected, of old Moylan. Dawnay was secretly amused at the idea: plum, staid Moylan with his catlike smile under the beard was certainly no sexual threat.

Dawnay watched as his wife chatted interminably, laughing, arguing, gesturing, sometimes serious, sometimes amused, sometimes mischievous, while Moylan allowed all the verbiage to wash over him, enjoying his secret smile and never having to say anything. Like so many writers, he preferred to digest, to observe, to take in, rather than to give out.

Dawnay chatted with Dafydd about his next book. His third novel—his second had

77

had a modest success and had made him ambitious—was to be about a group of student friends who hadn't seen each other in years, who set out on an exotic trip; he had an elaborate characterisation and plot about how much they had changed, how they screwed each other's girlfriends, and so on. The plot was too elaborate for Dawnay, as he half-listened to it. That was why he had wanted Dafydd to meet Moylan. The older man was good on taut, clever plots; he might be able to hose Dafydd's plot down, or offer suggestions on it.

Dawnay drew Moylan into the after-dinner conversation, explaining Dafydd's ideas to him. Moylan looked typically detached and noncommital. 'It's a good idea. It could work. Yes, I can see how it might be made to work. But you don't want to have Edward—that's the lawyer's name, isn't it—falling in love with the hippie's girlfriend. That wouldn't be true to character.'

'That's precisely what appeals to me about it,' said Dafydd. 'It's unexpected. It's the wild card in human nature that excites me, the unpredictable. Getting the relationship portrayed convincingly will be one of the challenges of the book.'

'Yes, but it also makes the whole situation overly complex, confusing.'

'I've never been able to get through one of your books for their complexity. If you don't mind me saying so.'

Moylan turned pink and smiled. 'Not at all.' But it was clear that he did mind—very much. An embarrassed hush fell upon them.

'But,' cut in Dawnay, whose attention had been far away, 'the whole point of your last book, Dafydd, was that it was so startlingly simple. Such a straight, powerful theme. You don't want to confuse your readers.'

'The critics said it was unoriginal. That it had no plot, no invention, no twists.'

'To hell with the critics. It sold well,' said Sarah's voice from the far sofa. Dawnay hadn't noticed the lull in her conversation with the other two women. She was being helpful.

Dafydd's clear brow furrowed. 'Maybe.'

'Why don't we all write one big novel together, each of us contributing three chapters,' said Sarah grandly. 'We can all write. I used to be a journalist. You used to write the best of letters when we were kids, remember, Pen?' she said to her sister. 'I'm sure even you can write,' she said to Moylan's wife, irking both her and her husband. In twenty-two years of marriage, Dawnay hadn't been able to get used to her directness; the diplomat in him, he supposed. Still, it often did more good than harm; he guessed that their friends were more amused by her lively charm than by his careful social manoeuvering. 'The only really dull writer here is Willie. That's what comes of writing despatches.' They all laughed.

'It might jar a little with your breathless, one-word-a-sentence *Time* style,' said Dawnay dryly, and they laughed, although less easily, because no one could ever tell from Dawnay's expression whether he was being serious or not: The twitch at the edge of his mouth was too slight.

But his eyes sparkled at Sarah, and she knew. 'I always said you should have been a photographer. That way I couldn't have said anything about your pictures, and you couldn't have said anything about my writing,' she exclaimed. God, how Dawnay loved her; he was terribly dependent on her, he knew. When Jill had died, there had been a danger that he would plunge, spinning, into a vortex of depression so deep he couldn't get out. Instead, she had forced him to climb out of the pit, leaving his self-pity and self-hatred behind him. She had bullied him and encouraged him and loved him and focused his attention away from al-Dawah. She had forced him into the new job, she had bought the house for them, she had given her friends to him—how few he had, he remembered, after more than a year abroad. He looked at the flush in her cheeks, the sensuousness and voluptuousness of her figure, even at her age, and he envied her desperately her energy, and he was glad she had given him so much. She was his life; and she made up for the dullness and dreariness of his work, of the office hours—

What had got into him? He enjoyed his work. It was this bloody business of the typescript that was getting him down. That, and this peculiar bug he had contracted, which left him low and debilitated and had puzzled his doctor too. He wasn't feeling that brilliant even now. He felt hot and shivery by turns, although not as badly as when he had the flu. He glanced across at Dafydd, now talking animatedly to Sarah. He envied the young man for his certainty, for his assurance, for his optimism. He hadn't reached the age of disappointment, of struggling to survive, but he would. Dawnay decided then that he had nothing to envy Dafydd, for the hard times were still ahead of him. God, he was having a lot of maudlin thoughts; it must be the whisky that was getting to him. He had drunk four in the last hour.

The Moylans made their excuses fairly early and left. She seemed to have enjoyed herself, over-enthusing as usual about the evening. 'You must come and see us soon. We've been redecorating at home for months, so we haven't seen anyone, we've had no social life at all.' Moylan himself, with that grin that said nothing, had to half-pull her through the door.

The evening had not gone too badly, but it hadn't served its purpose. Dafydd hadn't wanted to have his book interfered with, while Moylan had evidently taken a dislike to the argumentative young man, and would need a lot of persuading to get involved. Oh well, it all boiled down to personality eventually.

Dawnay went back to where Dafydd, Sarah and her sister were having a drink. Dafydd was lit up with drink, by now talking animatedly, laughing, his expression conveying his meaning, his hands working as hard. Both the women seemed to enjoy letting the young man talk. Dawnay did, too. He filled up their glasses.

The young man turned to him, without realising that his manner had become aggressive. They had been—inevitably—talking about literature. 'Willie, you're a publisher. Fuck it, you must know there's no objectivity to it! You just publish what you damn well like. Or what you think works well. It's your guess. You can't know.'

'I can't know. But I've a pretty good idea. Of course there's such a thing as objectivity. Don't tell me there's no difference between *Wuthering Heights* and a *Mills and Boon,* or that one can't tell the difference.'

'Hell no. Not at the time. *Wuthering Heights* was just the *Mills and Boon* of its age,' insisted the young man.

Dawnay couldn't prevent himself from snorting. Sarah rushed to Dafydd's defence. 'He's got a point. It was just considered entertainment, not in the class of Dickens or Trollope.'

'You've got it the wrong way round, my dear,' said Dawnay silkily. 'Dickens was entertainment, published in magazine instalments. *Wuthering Heights* was recognised for the masterpiece it was the moment it was published—'

And so it went on: just a standard literary dinner-party conversation. Just like the diplomatic circuit ones, reflected Dawnay, except more relaxed, more informal, with more intelligent, less catty people. But in the end there was the same snobbery about literary knowledge, the same discussions that went around in circles. All human society was much the same—in an embassy, an officers' mess, a private house. He sipped his drink. Of them all, he preferred the literary scene. He was steeped in it now, it was his space, his life, he didn't want it disrupted... Damn, why didn't his mind stop returning to that bloody book!

It was past one before he could get Dafydd out; Sarah's sister left at the same time, though in a different taxi. After they had closed the front door, Sarah put an arm round him. 'I thought you were a little tired tonight.'

'It's this bug.' He wasn't going to tell her about the book, he'd made up his mind about that—desperately as he wanted to share the burden, to be comforted.

'Poor darling. Why not take tomorrow off?'

'No, there's one manuscript I absolutely must finish.'

Yet he did take the day off. He went to the doctor first. He was feeling more like his usual self in the morning, and was reasonably clear-headed when he descended the front steps.

He wasn't prepared for the gravity of the doctor's expression. Mind, the doctor had always been rather a grave, sepulchral man, with a face as long as a horse's, huge cavernous eyes that spelt sadness, and great ears like flags at half mast. The old man always wore a dark suit. Yet he had a self-mocking humour, as though he knew how he appeared, and Dawnay had always found him professionally excellent. The humour was absent now. He seemed to be choosing his words carefully as he spoke to his patient.

'You're suffering from some rather classical symptoms, I'm afraid. They're nothing to worry about. In terms of serious disease, nothing at all—but I'm afraid the symptoms are quite unpleasant, and could take some time to go away.'

'Please be to the point, John. I am adult—if not quite as old as you are.' Dawnay had got away with this kind of banter in the past.

The doctor looked at his hands, and kept well off the point. 'Chemically, one's body undergoes some changes as one gets older. These—transition periods—don't last long. But they can be very unpleasant. They can induce disturbance in the pattern of sleep, of diet, of personal feelings. You are in fact suffering from depression, which as I say is a chemical, not a psychological state. But it can be caused psychologically, and of course has serious psychological consequences—which should pass reasonably quickly. But I'm going to prescribe some pills which should help a little.'

Dawnay had been prescribed the pills before, after Jill's death. He remembered his feelings then—and he prayed that he would not have to cross that dangerous sea again. 'But what's caused it, Doctor?'

'Can't say at the moment. We've done plenty of tests, and should get the results soon enough. It could be a viral infection. It could be some sort of poisoning. Or it could have been psychologically caused. If it's psychological, you'll have to look to yourself for the answer. But, as I say, it may be a simple virus.'

Dawnay left shaken. It couldn't have been the book—he had had the symptoms before it ever loomed on his horizon.

TWO

The road wound like a tiny thin ribbon down a steep incline into a vast plain, enclosed on one side by a row of mountains like the rim of a saucer, on the other ending in a foreshortened horizon, where it dropped 11,000 feet to the sea. All of that plain was grey, bare, sparsely vegetated, empty except for a small town perched high on a hill in the shimmering distance. They hadn't passed any other cars on the road now for some time: the road was reported to have been mined in places, and people travelled as little as they could these days, as the rebels advanced.

I had experienced a strange sensation at the beginning of the journey, a feeling not just of apprehension and fear, but of enjoyment of these emotions. It was exciting going into potentially dangerous land. But that feeling had been overtaken by one of fascination with the magnificence of the landscape, its emptiness, the way the road was the only evidence of the twentieth century in the whole of that wilderness. And crossing the valley floor I longed to reach the edge, the lip, to where it plunged towards the sea.

A hand grasped my elbow. 'No need to be alarmed, my dear. I've been down here six times in a year and nothing's happened yet. Of course the road isn't mined: the rebels need it to get their equipment up from the south and they need the supply lorries from the north they're always hijacking. Don't worry—they won't hijack us. It all happens—oh, at least eighty kilometres further south. The army gets its supplies down there in those old props you see coming banging in and out of al-Dawah. They don't need the road.'

I wished David Pugh would stop talking. He had been a ceaseless chatterer all the way down, and one had to take one's gaze away from the scenery to make occasional replies to the things he said. He seemed to imagine we were all terrified, except himself. He was the man of war, and it was his territory we were driving into. I wished I could have told him that the romance of this strange plateau, this country unchanged for thousands of years, was a perfume far headier than the stale smells of exploded shells. He had insisted I sit in front, sandwiched between him and the driver. I was glad in a way, because there I had a general view of the whole wild panorama unravelling. But I had to put up with him. In the back, conversation had long since ceased.

We rose up to a slight edge of the plateau, and then we were over, and I gazed rapt on the crags that crashed down, in a jagged line, towards green far, far, below. The fall was interrupted by occasional outcrops, by soaring, mysterious villages perched impossibly on little shelves by the long ribbon of road zig-zagging its way down the cliffs. The valley was so far down, it could only be discerned through the haze. I wanted to weep at the majesty of it all.

'Down there,' said David, pointing, 'that's Umlat. That's our watering hole.'

His wife in the back had awakened. 'But

don't drink the water there, whatever you do. You'll catch yellow fever at once!' She pealed with laughter, jarringly.

'We're well prepared for that, my dear. Scotch, wine, beer—you name it! A hamper full—'

'Don't people object to alcohol in as remote a place as this? It's not like the bar of the Taj Mahal, after all,' I wondered out loud.

'My goodness, we can't change our habits to fit in with theirs,' said Mrs Pugh. 'We'd all be going native next.'

'They've never seen alcohol, they won't even know what we're doing. Anyway, we're not stopping in the town itself. There's a lovely spot by the river down there, where the wheat grows over your head—I thought we'd go there,' said her husband.

'They're all high on chewing qat. Why should they object to a far less intoxicating habit?' put in Willie, taking their side as usual.

'There doesn't seem to be much sign of your war here,' I said to David, changing the subject.

'That's what I've been telling you. The action's further south. The rebels hold the

90

country twenty miles south of Umlat, I haven't seen hide nor hair of them on the way.'

'Or of anyone, for that matter,' said Willie.

'Bears out what I've always said about this bloody war,' said the colonel. 'It's not going to get anywhere.'

'Don't speak too soon,' I said with a laugh.

'Darling, don't worry!' said Mrs Pugh, with her awful patronising laugh.

We stopped, as David had said we would, a few miles outside the city, down a rough track off the road, which had curved its way through the thick yellow wheatfields down to a blissfully green-grassed slope—so green it could have been England. The country down here, along the coastal belt, was lush and verdant by comparison with the stony, bare mountainous plateau above. The river—it was really just a big stream, although quite deep for a torrent that could have been no more than nine feet across—sauntered down beneath the date palms that dotted the green bank. It was an incongruous mixture of vegetation and climate, and yet it was extremely beautiful.

When we reached our picnic spot, I wanted to rush out of the car, to lay down beneath the tree, as in the England I remembered; it came as a shock to be greeted with the furnace blast of heat of an al-Dawah autumn. In the shade it was just cool enough to sit out, though, to eat and drink.

The car was out of sight, behind a hillock. The driver kept watch on it—just in case. Colonel Pugh was jovial but I noticed a faint uneasiness in the way he kept looking around, as though he was aware of his duty to protect us, as the only soldier among us and the person who had said it was safe to come.

His wife sufferered from no such inhibition. She prattled away—mostly to Willie, because she could see that I wasn't interested; her husband grinned dutifully at her jokes, although he had heard them all before. She wore a long khaki skirt to halfway down her calves, and a plain white shirt with plenty of room in it, so that the air could cool her arms and breasts, where they moved firmly under the loose material. She would have been a good-looking woman—she must have been at least forty—but for the way her hair was done up too conventionally, to make her look older. The smile, also, was too fixed, the lips somehow welded in a grimace onto her face.

Willie lay spread out a little further away in the grass in his light grey canvas trousers and open white shirt. He laughed a lot at her jokes, and drank a lot. He was by turns moody and jokey. I didn't care. I was in a reverie, gazing at the yellow of the cornfields and the green of the river bank and the grey-blue of the river and the deep blue of the sky and the fuzzy grey of the mountains in the distance. I could think of no more perfect place in the world.

After lunch, even the eternal burbler had had enough. Her sleep was interrupted only by the colonel, who announced that he was going into town to chat with the local elders, to find out where the rebels were. We were perfectly safe, he assured us. After he had gone, Willie came and sat down beside me. 'What's the matter?' he asked irritably.

'Nothing. What's the matter with you?'

'For God's sake, Jill.' He always called me Jill when he was angry. Otherwise it was darling, or love, or Jay. 'You've

93

been absolutely bloody all the way here. You wouldn't even turn to look at David Pugh.'

'I didn't notice you talking a great deal.'

'I was in the back, for God's sake. These people have gone to a lot of trouble to organise this outing, and you behave like a bored, spoilt brat.'

'Would it surprise you to know that I have loved every minute of it? That I am enchanted with the place? Absolutely enchanted.'

'Really?' He looked sceptical.

'It's just he's always giving a running commentary on everything. He's such a bore.'

'Good God. You call him a bore. Who are you anyway to be rude to people like the Pughs?'—he stopped short.

'Yes? Go on: "They're a lot more amusing than you are" is what you were going to say.'

'Yes, if you want to know.'

I was determined to keep my temper. The tears fought their way out, though, from under my eyelids. He looked hard at me. I knew he couldn't bear to see me crying, but he didn't want to surrender

94

either. I couldn't care less. I hated him at that moment. The frustration of months was spilling out. The frustration at the way he preferred his new friends to me, with all their ghastly snobbery and bitchiness. He had joined them. He had taken their side against me. He seemed to regard me as a handicap, a social cripple. I did my best in the dinner party circuit, but what they said bored me, and I couldn't think of anything to say, and I knew they didn't like me anyway. I couldn't do more than my best.

He put an arm around me. 'That was a bit strong. I didn't mean it. It's just—well, I wish you would try just a little more.'

'But why must I try? Why can't I do what I want, instead of what they want? I want to lead my own life! They should try more with me.'

'But they do, that's the point. Meet them halfway. Compromise.' I couldn't help it: I burst into tears and wept on his shoulder, and he held me close, and it was all over. But it wasn't, of course.

I lay in the shade, savouring the heat. I had pulled my skirt halfway up my thighs but I didn't dare go any further, in case some

Islamic-minded peasant happened by. The scene was perfectly tranquil. Willie had passed out beside me: he had drunk too much at lunch. The colonel's wife was looking bored, without Willie to prattle to. She had taken to reading a book—one of those rather risqué novels about spies by the author they were all talking about, Ian Fleming. I decided to go for a walk.

'I'm going to look at the town. David said it was only a couple of miles down the road.'

'You'll get frazzled in this heat,' said Willie, opening an eye. 'And then there's the guerrillas—'

'You aren't coming?'

'Not likely.'

'Cowardy custard.' So I set off on my own.

He was right. The road wound interminably through the cornfields and there was no sign of the town: you could have been miles from anywhere. The heat out in the sun was overpowering. Before I'd gone a quarter of a mile I wondered if I should turn back. And being all alone out there made me suddenly nervous. It was easy, in the company of English people, to forget that I was in a strange, very primitive country thousands of miles from England. Anything could happen—even an assault from an Islamic fanatic, and there were many in al-Dawah, who would be infuriated at the sight of a woman with no headscarf. And then I thought of all those daring Englishwomen who had crossed the world decades before me, and I went on. The town couldn't be far.

I reached a corner of the road and there it was, framed on one side of a small hill. It looked like old Jerusalem, or a little crib of Bethlehem I had been given as a child. Unpaved streets merged with dark alley entrances up the hill; houses perched precariously, as they always seemed to in al-Dawah, along the hillsides. Two magnificent domed mosques with minarets punctuated the disorganised skyline of roofs all in a jumble.

I thought it enchanting, even as I made my way up the first row of steps that led to the first of the streets, where the stench of the open drains running down the side of the tracks hit me. It smelt awful, but looked beautiful. The women glanced at me from behind their face scarves, then lowered their eyes, as though they had seen an obscenity. I found their shawls—spectacular displays of purple, red, blue and white—staggering. The men looked straight at me, curiously. Some stopped in their tracks. I knew that only a prostitute went around with uncovered head. I didn't care. I was too taken by what I saw.

The little streets towards the top of the town were quieter, after I had pushed through a small but bustling market. There I gazed down from beside a mosque with a gold-topped dome into the little horse-shoe-shaped valley that Umlat was at the end of. The cornfields curved peacefully away into the distance, cradling the river. Far away the hazy grey of the mountain range could be seen. I watched entranced in that peaceful place for twenty minutes, recovering from the heat and the stares and the effort of making my way there.

I was startled by the English voice beside me. 'You were very silly to come here alone, you know. Anything might have happened.'

It was Colonel Pugh. His voice was surprisingly gentle, not its usual gruff bark or jollier-than-thou megaphone. It also expressed concern.

'I can look after myself, thank you,

David,' I replied, a little coolly.

'Well, I suppose you have.' He smiled. 'But it's more worrying than I thought. There's been fighting at Ibb-al-Said, to the north there.' He pointed. 'Eight government soldiers killed and twenty-eight civilians. The local chiefs here have managed to strike a deal with the guerrillas. They won't harbour any soldiers here, and in return the guerrillas leave them alone. The local chiefs here have got a militia of their own—the central government can't impose its will on them—but Ibb was too small for that. The guerrillas moved in and put the little garrison to rout. They took reprisals against the villagers. Oh, it's all small-scale stuff, I know. The government soldiers were caught by surprise. But that's how these wars are fought.'

'Were you always interested in war, Colonel?'

He reddened. 'Yes. And it is a fascinating subject. Doesn't mean one likes the bloodiness that goes with it.' He changed the subject. 'Beautiful view, isn't it.'

'Yes,' I said, quietly and with feeling.

'D'you mind me saying,' he cleared his throat, 'that you're a beautiful girl.'

I was so surprised I blushed furiously.

'No. Not at all,' I smiled.

And then he did it, with all the clumsiness of his profession. He took my two shoulders in his hands, and pulled me towards him. The fat lips, the red face, the moustache descended before I had time to move. I experienced his moisture, his tongue, the smell of his breath before I was able to struggle free. 'I'm sorry, I'm sorry, I'm not—' I was furious, I didn't know what to say. 'You're more primitive than any of them!' I let out angrily.

He cleared his throat, dusted himself down, looked very brisk and military and stern, backing off all the time. 'Yes. Ah well, I see. Well, we'd better be going back to the others now.'

Without speaking we set off towards the lower streets. We didn't even look at each other. Suddenly he stopped. 'You didn't—you didn't mind what happened, did you,' he asked nervously.

I had recovered some of my composure. 'No. Really. I was flattered. It's just that I don't believe in betraying my husband.' I knew it would reinforce my reputation as a prig, and I didn't care.

'You won't mention this to anyone, will you?'

'Of course not,' I said. He seemed relieved. By the time we were on the road out of town, he was his old self again, talking loudly about everything.

We made our way through the wheatfield. I was longing for a cool drink by now; the heat had been too intense for too long, but luckily the sun was beginning to fade in the late afternoon. The scene was very still.

I think I caught sight of the body before he did. I stopped, rooted to the spot. My tension communicated itself to him: he stopped too, and followed my gaze. The car, a little dust barely smudging its beautifully polished chrome, lay inert where it had been parked, the driver's door hanging half open. On the stony, dusty ground beside it lay the body of the driver, drained of all life. He was on his back, his arms splayed behind him.

'My God!' breathed David. 'Down,' he whispered, recovering his professional poise instantly. He was urgent now, a man of action. And in the terror that had gripped me, I instantly obeyed. He knew what he was doing. 'Where did you leave the others?'

'On the riverbank, where we had the

picnic,' I whispered. 'Do you think—?' The fear had reached my throat, almost paralysing speech. I was dry and weak with the possibility that Willie...

'I don't know. But I should worry about yourself first, before worrying about them. Come on,' he beckoned. Slowly, cautiously, we made our way back through the corn, straining to hear every noise about us. There was nothing, even though we paused for a while to listen. I didn't have time to analyse my own feelings, although next to the sense of panic there was one of excitement. It was terribly uncomfortable, running half-crouched through the corn, sweat coming from every pore, our legs cramped because of the posture. We reached the riverbank in minutes—but it seemed like ages—to witness a more terrible sight still—one which so astonished us that for seconds we just gazed. It was the precise opposite of what we were expecting to see.

Twenty yards from us, upon a hump of thick grass just under the tree, a pair of boots was dug into the ground, toes downwards. On either side a bare foot pointed upwards. Above that were grey trousers ending prematurely in a jumble of cloth and an undone belt; above that, scrawny naked thighs blended into scrawny naked buttocks that I thought I recognised. That was all that could be seen. The animal was moving, up and down, up and down, rhythmically. The noise it emitted was that of a woman panting happily. 'Oh yes, oh yes, oh yes.'

It took me seconds even to begin to understand what I was seeing, I was so astounded. After that my fear, tension, excitement gradually boiled into anger. Like a cat, I prepared to pounce. Only a hand—a hand with a vice-like grip on my arm—stopped me. 'Don't be such a bloody fool. They could still be around. They've killed one man already. That's more important than—than this,' he hissed. I allowed myself to be fixed to the spot. He glanced at me to see if I really was under control, and said, 'Stay here.' He moved cautiously on his haunches, like a frog, inching as close to the couple as the shelter allowed.

I watched for the next few moments as if in a trance, in which I had suspended all feeling because that was the only way of keeping a hold on myself. Later, I told myself, later he would pay. If there was to be a later. David suddenly loomed up over them. They hadn't noticed his approach. The single unit separated into two like an organism reproducing itself. It should have been funny, quite uproariously funny, but it didn't seem so to me.

From my ringside seat I watched Willie, embarrassed and alarmed and—I'm afraid to say—scared of the colonel, pulling up his trousers, buttoning himself up, tucking in the shirt he had never removed. I watched her, cool as a cucumber, pulling down the skirt that had been ruffed up to her waist, taking up her discarded underwear and jamming it into a bag, putting on her sandals. She eased her ruffled hair back into place, to regain her dignity, with an expression of injured innocence. She began to say—she had the cheek to say—'Really, David, don't you think you could behave more discreetly—' and I heard him whisper, 'For God's sake, Daphne, the guerrillas have got the driver.' That silenced her.

I couldn't bear to be with them as we made our way back to the car, to where the body lay. As I crawled forward to join David, I exchanged one look with Willie and I could read the shock in his face, and I hated him—hated him! He could read that too. It took about ten minutes before we were close to the clearing where the car was. The scene was unchanged, the body still splayed out in the sun. David said 'We've got to pray they're not still about. I'm going to see if the car's in working order.'

A moment later, a peal of loud, silly laughter stopped us all in our tracks.

'For God's sake, Dawnay!' boomed the military attaché. Willie was on his feet rocking with laughter. The colonel leapt up, grabbed Willie, and knocked him down into the corn. 'Dammit man, you've given our position away.'

'It's qat,' spluttered Willie.

'What?'

'Qat. The bloody man's as tight as a tick in qat.' Qat was the weed that al-Dawaians chewed to their hearts' content to make them forget the boredom of life. It was mildly narcotic, a long thin leaf. It had become the country's main crop, surpassing their coffee, which had been their traditional export. 'He brought a bundle of leaves as thick as your arm. He's been chewing it all afternoon. He offered some to us. We tried it, it made us feel good, and a bit funny too. He passed out an hour ago.'

Willie walked past the astonished colonel to the body. He kicked it gently. The body stirred, the face assuming an inane grin. 'Wake up, Ahmed, wake up,' barked Willie. The little man climbed to his feet using the car for support. He was sheepish, unhappy, smiling desperately, his crime found out. He staggered over to the car, barely capable of movement, he was still so drugged.

David rose to his full height, six foot three, his face pained, humiliated and, as always red. 'Well, thank God for that at least,' was all he said. His wife for once looked subdued; a middle-aged woman, her hair still ruffled, she was ashamed of herself and tight-lipped. Willie was still laughing gently, his hands on his hips.

I moved forward, faced him and slapped him on the side of his face as hard as I could. His expression clouded over to one of bleak fury, but he didn't react, and I walked over to the car, by now oblivious to the reaction of other people. The return journey took place in nearly total silence.

Looking back on it, dear Willie, it was all

so silly. I suppose one should have a sense of humour about these things. What a good story it made: diplomats caught with their trousers down in a far-off country. Now that one is older, one knows that married men in small, closed societies break out by sleeping with the wives of their colleagues. In saying no to David I was just branding myself a prig. I was breaking an unwritten rule of diplomatic life abroad....

You, Willie, merely fulfilled your role, and had a little fun besides. Who can blame you for not wanting a quick screw with a different woman, when it was offered to you on a plate? She wasn't unattractive, even if a little old for you. Add to these two silly, perfectly normal affairs between diplomatic colleagues—one consummated, one not—the fact that the driver passes out drugged and we assume the guerillas have killed him—and you have a splendidly funny story for the diplomatic circuit. All so amusing and undramatic, in the end.

But I couldn't see the joke. I gave you hell that evening. And then didn't speak to you for days. I couldn't help it: Irrational feelings had taken over. You had soiled yourself with that bitch. You had in one afternoon degraded our relationship—how could you be in love with

*me if you could do that with someone else?
And to do it with the woman in the embassy
you knew I most despised. I hated you, I hated
you, I hated you!*

*It was only as my anger subsided that I
began to realise how much you despised me.*

*It wasn't in the way you behaved in
private. From trying to make up to me in
the first few days, from being shameful and
abashed, you became hurt and withdrawn and
miserable, which actually softened me towards
you. It was the way you behaved at functions,
distancing yourself from me. Remember the
National Day parade, and the cocktail party
at the embassy that evening, which the Sultan
attended—the only diplomatic reception he
visited on such a prestigious day? What a
fillip that gave to those whose life depended
on such trivia!*

It was only a week after the great riverbank
affair. It was the first time the four of
us—we had gone to great lengths to avoid
each other—had been thrown together since
then. H.E was the front ranker at the
parade. David had to go because he was
military attaché; and Willie went because
H.E wanted him to keep an eye out for
the political implications of the parade.

There was a special dais for ambassadors, next to the dais where the Sultan and his ministers took the salute. The main street of the capital had been blocked off to traffic, and the daises erected to protect the official spectators from the overpowering sun. One embassy car had deposited H.E and his wife, another ourselves, yet another the Pughs; the drivers roared off, as they liked to do on important occasions, raising dust that covered those who were watching from behind the stiff line of police.

We took our seats uncomfortably alongside the Pughs, exchanging fixed smiles. David said, heartily, 'It's my day really. I do a report on the new equipment that goes past. Usually there isn't any. This time—we should see something. They won't resist putting it on show, even though it tells the whole world and any damn intelligence agent in the place just what they've got; the message gets back to the rebels at once.'

'These parades are the most frightful bore,' said Daphne, at her most exaggerated. 'I've watched two of them now. Exactly the same, every time. And the dust is simply frightful. My dear,' she added to me, 'how well you look.'

The significance of this remark escaped me. I smiled coldly and turned to stare ahead. Willie seemed eager to make up for my rudeness. He exchanged pleasantries with the Pughs at every break in the parade. I watched, fascinated, as the marchpast began. There were men dressed in Arab headgear and British-style brown uniforms, mounted on white horses. They were followed by the infantry and by an array of jeeps and very antique-looking artillery. Looking sideways, I could glimpse the ruling troika: the short, slender young Sultan, his hair dark and curling, his face locked in an expression of fixed, boyish seriousness as he stood rigid at attention. Beside him was Salim Haddad, his elderly prime minister, a tall man grown stooped with age, his head bowed and blending into a rather sagging chin, his mouth a long thin line across the lower half of his face, his nose arched a little, his eyes small, brittle and alert. He looked weary with responsibility and power, yet not a man to be trifled with. His suit was dark, perfectly tailored.

On the Sultan's other flank was Hafez al-Ashraf, the armed forces commander, a tall, trim young military figure with golden epaulettes, gold braid and a chestful of ribbons. He flashed a brilliant smile under his Clark Gable moustache from time to time. He looked tough and jovial. He alone of the three saluted.

The parade lasted two hours; there was a short flypast by the air force's four twin-propeller aircraft. And then it was over. David turned pleasantly to us, saying, 'You must come back and have a drink with us. We've also asked a few of my colleagues.'

'We'd love to,' said Willie without hesitation. I was furious. He was suggesting that the incident had been forgotten, a thing of the past. But I hadn't forgotten. And besides, I hated military parties. This one was just as I expected: a lot of loud-talking, stupid men with their flashing teeth, firm jaws, easy smiles, chiselled looks and braying accents. And a lot of blowsy women shouting at each other. They were like peacocks, all dressed up in their finery, competing and showing off to each other.

Willie soon abandoned me. I was left talking to a rather polite, withdrawn woman, bearing an expression of distaste she only occasionally punctuated by set-piece party phrases. As neither of us was very forthcoming, we soon gave up the conversation and I found myself being taken up by the Italian military attaché, a well-built, slightly swarthy man whose lack of physical attraction he more than compensated for by charm. On the other side of the room, I had seen Willie dutifully making the round of the various attachés, moving inexorably towards Daphne Pugh. I lost all interest in what the Italian was saying as I watched Willie's face shine as she greeted him.

And then I had a flash of inspiration. I had to compete with her, not to push Willie further away from me by fighting him. I interrupted the Italian in full flow with a question about whether Capri was as beautiful as they said. 'Capri? Yes, of course.' He looked surprised. 'But there are more beautiful places. You mean you have never been to Italy?'

I detached myself politely. My mind made up, I made my own way towards David, starting up conversations with people I didn't know. Some responded, some didn't. I couldn't care less. I asked them where they came from, where they lived, how they liked the country. Boring questions, but they seemed happy enough to respond. I was flushed with social success; feeling rather pleased with myself, I reached David. 'What a marvellous party,' I said.

'Yes, I thought you were enjoying it.' He was bearing a champagne bottle and refilled my glass. I smiled at him. My eyes looked rather teasing. He smiled uneasily.

'You know, I enjoyed our visit to Umlat.'

'Really?' His expression looked strained. 'Didn't seem so at the time.'

'No, I mean when we visited the town itself.' He glanced around as though he thought I was trying to embarrass him. 'I never give in first time. Men prefer a chase.'

This time he grinned broadly, and then recovered himself. 'I'll remember that,' he said, as he passed on with the champagne bottle.

I had been drinking all day by the time the embassy evening party began, and must have seemed slightly uncertain as I walked up the steps in my best dress, a long cream one with elegant shoulder straps that widened out to cover my bosom, while permitting a falling neckline that for a diplomatic party was downright daring. Willie hummed and hawed about whether or not I should wear it, at length relenting. When we got there, I could see the disapproving gaze of the older women. One or two of the men cast furtive, approving looks.

I found myself talking to H.E early on. He was nervous. 'It's a tremendous honour, the Sultan visiting, you know. I hope he doesn't arrive too late.'

'All the guests will stay for him,' I reminded him.

'That's true,' he said. 'How are you enjoying life down here?'

'Very much,' I said, with as much conviction as I could muster.

'Settling in all right?'

'Yes.'

'Good, good.' He still looked hesitant, as if he wanted to add something else.

He glanced over my shoulder. 'Sorry. Duty calls.' He went out towards the front door, to greet the royal party. We all fell into a line that had been carefully arranged beforehand to greet the Sultan. He was dressed in the ubiquitous long white tunic of his country; a charming smile, polished by years of use, was flashed at each person. His eyes positively gleamed with friendliness. He shook hands almost perfunctorily, barely allowing his palm to rest in another's hand. Willie murmured something, then the Sultan reached me and stopped. I tried desperately to think of something to say. He obliged. 'You have been in my country a long time?'

'Five months, Your Royal Highness.'

'And what do you think of it?'

'I love it. The old city especially. We have a flat there.'

His eyebrows shot up. 'You live in the old city? That's remarkable—very few of my own people stay: they all save up to move out. But I agree with you. The old city has more life. It is close to the heart of the country. I am always close to the heart of my people.' His accent was mostly upper-class English.

'I imagine that you travel a great deal to meet your people,' I said. The newspapers were always full of pictures of the Sultan's visits.

The ambassador smiled politely beside him. 'This is Peter Donovan, the consul,' he began.

But the Sultan would not be moved on. 'I believe I must be close to them,' he said earnestly. 'I must never lose touch with them. They are a very good people. Living where you do you will have seen that. In the old city they live as they really are; they are not trying to impress. They are a simple, virtuous people.'

'Very devout too,' I said, for want of anything else to say.

He looked suddenly very serious and intense. 'You are right. Very devout, very Islamic. That is the most important thing of all. Devout in their personal lives, because their personal lives must always be guided by the Prophet. But there are people that will try to manipulate their devotion to their own ends, and that cannot be tolerated. This must be a modern country. Religion and the state must be separate. That is the law in your country, is it not? The same applies here. What can prayer leaders know of how a country should be run, of what it needs: new roads, housing, electricity generation? Why, such people would try to forbid me talking to you, because you are a woman and your face is unveiled. They are barbarians, living in the past.'

'But surely such people are a tiny minority?' asked the ambassador.

The Sultan flashed a brilliant, cold smile at him. 'Of course,' he said. He turned back to me. 'You must come and visit me,' he said, glancing at Willie. 'Both of you.' He proceeded regally down the line. We closed up with the others.

'Christ almighty,' breathed Willie furiously. 'Did you have to go prattling on at him like that?'

I was taken aback. 'He was talking to me.'

'Yes, but you should have just let him glide by. I'm in for it—' Hugo and David and Daphne came up.

'Poor boy,' said Daphne. 'He looked so hopelessly out of his depth. I expect he enjoyed talking to you.'

'Wonder how long he'll last,' said David.

Hugo, who had been standing next to Willie, butted in, smiling encouragingly at me. 'I thought what he said was bloody interesting. I'm glad you got that out of him about the Islamic problem. It's on his mind alright.'

'Yes, the deputy defence minister, Abdul Rashid, was telling me all about it only the other day,' said Daphne.

'It's a lot of nonsense,' said her husband. 'It's those damn radicals and their friends in the National Liberation Front that are the problem.'

The same old endless conversation. And yet the Sultan clearly had felt strongly about what he said.

Willie returned to the attack the moment we were driving away. 'Next time you want to make a fool of me, do it with someone a little less obvious than the Sultan.'

'Fool of you! He wanted to talk to me. I just answered him, that's all. If I hadn't there would have been a diplomatic incident.'

'There has been one, and I'm the one who takes the rap.' He was almost speechless with rage.

'What are you talking about?' I was contemptuous.

'David had a word in my ear,' he snapped out angrily.

'What did he say. What has he got to do with me?'

'If you want to know, he said I should keep you on a tighter rein. That what you did just isn't done.'

'What right has that bloody man to tell me anything—?'

'Look Jill, an embassy is a hierarchical

place: there are lines of importance and precedence and seniority. God willing, if we ever rise to ambassadorial status we're allowed to talk to Sultans. But not before then. You broke a rule. It's like the army. God, you don't understand anything, do you?'

'You're the slave of the system. Not me. I'm not paid by anyone.'

He looked hard at me and said, with a deep breath as if terminally exhausted, 'You're not much help as a wife, are you?'

'That's what you think, is it?'

'That's what everyone's saying.'

'Well, everyone can go to hell! And so can you if all you see me as is—your helper.' I turned away from him and gazed out of the car window, and the tears ran down my cheeks slowly, and no hands came to comfort me.

Dawnay eased the car into an empty parking space on the main street. The village of Buxton was a yellow-bricked Cotswold hamlet become an American-frequented beauty spot. The main street sloped steeply down a hill; it was lined with small *bijou* shops selling antiques and handicrafts. Thatched roofs added distinction; a bridge at the bottom added the final touch of rural quaintness. Bus-loads of tourists shambled up and down the pavements, gawking.

Dawnay left his car in gear as an additional precaution against the steepness of the slope, and walked the few yards to the pub. The day had begun as a sunny one, but had clouded over. He would be glad of a pint of beer. From the outside the pub looked like a country hostelry. Inside it was done up to the nines and very twee, with pewter mugs hanging in rows from the ceiling and every piece of furniture made of polished wood. Behind the bar a middle-aged woman with a busy smile fetched him a pint of lager. They didn't have bitters here, only tasteless English lager. She asked if he had booked.

'No, I'm just here for a drink,' he said.

'In that case you'll have to go into the bar, through there. This is for residents and those using the restaurant.' In the bar you could get bitters and there were rough wooden seats. Dawnay perched his lager on an empty table and bought a pint of bitter. Then he noticed that the man he had come to meet was already there.

The man started as he noted Dawnay. They moved towards each other simultaneously. 'Damn me, you haven't changed a lot!' exclaimed David Pugh with great warmth.

'Nor you,' said Dawnay, smiling. But he was lying. The transformation was astonishing. The once pink, full cheeks were hollow now, lined and stringy, concave around the bones. The eyes had huge hollows gouged underneath them. They were dull and without sparkle, with ragged grey eyebrows over them. Ragged was also the only way that the moustache could be described, although it still lent definition to a face which otherwise lacked it. His hair was very thin and greying. He looked eighty, although he could have been in his late sixties.

He was—or appeared to be—genuinely pleased to see Dawnay. 'Well, what do you think of it?'

'Of what?' asked Dawnay, startled.

'The town. Lovely, isn't it? I can understand why the tourists come up from London in droves to see it. I've always wanted to live here, ever since I was stationed down here at Madden

Camp. Marvellous place to retire to. Can I get you a drink?'

'No, no, it's mine. I asked you, remember,' said Dawnay. He had come prepared, a mask of conviviality locked into place.

Pugh wanted a double whisky. 'Middle of the day. The witching hour has come,' he said cheerfully. 'Marvellous idea of yours that we should have a get-together. It must be eighteen years.'

'Longer: twenty-two.'

'My goodness, how time flies.' He still talked in clichés, Dawnay noticed. 'I suppose you haven't seen much of the others recently?' he asked. 'You know, the old embassy crew from al-Dawah?'

'As a matter of fact, I ran into Hugo Hennessy only two days ago.'

'Good God,' he laughed. 'That old queen. I suppose he's taken up publishing with one of his own kind.'

Dawnay smiled. 'No, he's still in the service. Married. It's me that's taken up publishing now—although not, I hasten to add, with one of that kind. I've remarried.'

Pugh's eyes went up a millimetre. 'Really? You should have cherished your freedom, young man. I did. You probably don't know that Daphne left me—oh, ten years ago.'

Dawnay was astonished. He had considered them the perfectly complementary couple—Pugh cutting a fine dash, doing his duty, Daphne supremely helpful and socially accomplished. Now he noticed that the old man was chainsmoking. He didn't look happy. He wanted to talk. Dawnay didn't stop him. 'After that al-Dawah business, we were posted off to Iceland. Didn't enjoy that much, I can tell you. Cold and beastly country and there was nothing to do there. The Yanks looked after all the NATO side—the strategic side. We were just observers.' Dawnay nodded sympathetically. 'Well, you know, Daphne had a bit of a nervous breakdown after that al-Dawah business. She was always nervous, unsure of herself. She always envied your wife, you know, for her calmness. She was very fond of Jill.'

Dawnay nearly choked on his drink. He didn't say anything. The colonel looked at him, alarmed. 'She felt awfully guilty about what she had done to Jill, you know—well of course you know. Don't worry. I've long forgiven, if not forgotten. Had my own little temptations too, you know. Did you know I made a pass at Jill? She turned me down flat.'

'I know. She told me.'

He coloured. 'Did she? Well, to cut a long story short, for some silly reason it entered Daphne's head that she was partly responsible for what happened to Jill. That helped towards her breakdown. She recovered, of course, but her nerves were never quite the same. And we had always had our differences. She ran off with another soldier, some damn captain fifteen years younger than her, in Iceland. They've stuck together, so far as I know. Thank God we didn't have children.'

Dawnay suppressed a frown, then said slowly, thoughtfully. 'Why do you want me to know about all this?'

'Why? Don't really know. Don't see many people from the past these days. Only this little lot.' He waved his hand vaguely around the pub.

Dawnay felt almost sorry for him. 'I'd have liked to have seen Daphne again. She was full of fun, very lively, very amusing. Good in bed too.'

'Come on, man, what do you know—you only had her on the grass—'

Dawnay didn't like what he had to do.

'I'd been sleeping with her for more than a month before that happened. It was the end of the affair: We decided it wasn't worth the risk.'

Faint colour returned to dried-out veins in the colonel's cheeks. 'How dare you! You come here to see me in retirement to tell me this—'

'You mean you didn't know? Was that why you didn't include it in the book?'

The colonel's eyes bulged. 'Book? What the hell are you talking about?'

Dawnay looked at him long and hard. While reading the chapter on the outing to Umlat, his certainty had grown that this was the man. Pugh knew details that had only been known by Daphne and himself. No one else had been told about the episode on the riverbank. And he had motive. His divorce would have been enough to blight a senior military career, particularly one in diplomatic postings. Dawnay had wondered whether the affair years earlier could have been the start of the breakup. The colonel had just confirmed it. Besides, Pugh was obviously not a man of limitless means. His clothes were a rather shabby grey tweed jacket and baggy brown trousers. 'What makes you think publishers are rich?' asked Dawnay casually.

The colonel spoke in a clipped, brisk military tone. 'You are not talking sense, sir. I don't know anything about publishers, except that most of them are homosexual.' He was trying to get his own back now.

Dawnay was weary of going round in circles. 'Calm down, David.' He put a hand on the other's shoulder. 'I'll explain.' Dawnay reckoned he had nothing to lose by telling all.

By the time he had finished, the colonel was agog. 'Good God, what on earth's it all about?'

'That's what I keep asking myself.'

The colonel looked thoughtful. 'Mind if I get myself another whisky. Same again for you?' When he had returned from the bar, he asked, 'Do you believe it wasn't me now?'

'I'm not sure. I don't see why you'd do it. For that matter I don't think you could write that sort of book.'

'You're right about that. The most I can manage is a page to my son every few months.'

'But who else knew about the—the scene on the riverbank?'

126

'Unless Daphne told someone. I'm damn sure that neither of us did when we were in al-Dawah. Oh, I know we were the most frightful gossips. But Daphne was rather embarrassed about the whole thing.'

'Quennell? The ambassador? But how would they know?'

'Neither of them liked you, that's true. But Quennell—the man wouldn't punch his way out of a paper bag, let alone try something like this. And the ambassador—what motive would he have?' The colonel chuckled suddenly. 'It's awful for you, but my goodness, what a fascinating dilemma. But why do you think there's anything in the book to blackmail you about?'

'I don't know. I haven't found out. I just can't think of any other reason for writing such a thing.'

'You haven't finished it?' asked the colonel incredulously.

'I'm a slow reader.' The truth was that every word was like a pin stuck into him. He couldn't bring himself to read on.

'Come on, why don't you join me for a bite at home?' said the colonel, suddenly hearty. 'Harriet will be wondering where

I've got to. Didn't tell you I'd remarried, did I?'

The colonel was being bled white by his tough new wife and their two children, both in the midteens. Such money as he had was being creamed off by this girl, who had been a typist in the army camp he used to work in. She had a face as hard as nails, and barely concealed her contempt for the old man. She was pretty in a rather obvious way. Looking at the colonel, Dawnay couldn't imagine he had it in him to take what she had to offer.

The children were ghastly beyond belief: a brainless, horse-crazy lumpish girl of around fifteen with fair hair, a pudgy fresh face and a formless pubescent body. The boy was a bike-mad, surly youth with lank dark hair and a protruding lower jaw. They quarrelled across the table, ignoring the others. Dawnay made his excuses as soon as he decently could.

Standing by the car in front of the middle-sized farmhouse, Pugh said abruptly, 'You know, I was never one of those who thought you were responsible.'

'For what?'

'For Jill's death. But everyone else

thought you were. Go and see H.E. He's a man of many secrets.' Dawnay drove away from the scene of domestic confusion more muddled and depressed than before.

The ambassador. Dawnay remembered how his dislike of the man had grown quite steadily with every passing minute, in direct proportion to the dislike that the ambassador manifested towards him. After Dawnay's first three months in al-Dawah the ambassador was rather heavily editing his reports, toning them down. At H.E's morning meetings, which Dawnay would attend with Hennessy, Pugh and Quennell, H.E would politely ask each for his opinions of the issue of the day, but usually slap down Dawnay or cut him with a sarcastic remark.

Dawnay had not known at the time whether this was the normal way all junior embassy officers were treated; he assumed his advice would come to be accepted in time. Hugo, whom he saw little of socially, seemed to bear him no grudge. He occasionally tried to intervene in supporting Dawnay against

H.E. Sometimes Quennell also came down on his side. But H.E's practice of slapping down Dawnay had gone so far that he had come to retreat into a sullen silence at these conferences, so much so that the ambassador would sometimes ask him questions, to draw him out.

At one such meeting, he informed Dawnay that he had been granted an interview with Haddad. Would he like to come along? Dawnay remembered now how his hatred of the ambassador had flared into the open after that meeting. After it, Dawnay had hardly spoken civilly to him again. Now he would have to see him on a mission so delicate he hardly knew how to approach him to make the appointment.

Dawnay decided to stop the car at Oxford, on the way back from Pugh's house. He found a library to look up H.E's address in retirement in Who's Who. He imagined that H.E wouldn't be shy of advertising himself there. After finding it, he decided to spend the night in Oxford. The thought of going back to London, to the office, was too wearying while he was in his present state, with his nerves screaming for an end to the uncertainty, the mental agony. He went on to All Souls, of which he was a fellow. The place had its good points: he had the use of a room free. He put through a call to his secretary's home number, to say he was unwell and wouldn't be in next day. Then he put through another to Sandra Newell.

She sounded delighted. 'Willie! It's been years! What brings you to Oxford?'

'I just felt the urge to see you.'

'You were never that romantic. Or lustful. You always had to have a reason. What really brings you?'

'I'm on my way from meeting someone near Oxford. I just thought it would be nice to see you. You haven't anyone with you? You are free?'

'I'm always free for you. I don't know why. You're the most selfish person I know. But you know I can't resist you.'

'You've made me feel better already,' Dawnay said dryly. 'What about the Bunch of Grapes at eight o'clock?'

She said yes. That gave Dawnay two hours' reading time and time for a bath. He picked up the accursed thing, poured himself a whisky, and began reading.

THREE

The Friday Willie saw Haddad the heavens opened for the first time since we had arrived in al-Dawah. The day had really been stifling, oppressively hot. The clouds had flocked together in the late afternoon, over the low line of hills to the east of the capital. It seemed almost uncanny when the sun was blotted out over the capital in daytime, when the blue sky became grey, as though an eclipse had taken place. When the rain came it was in large drops that pattered around the house. Together with many other inhabitants, I went out of the flat and down into the street to experience the joyous washing sensation of the rain, of water from the skies.

I knew Willie would be late because of the meeting. He returned at eight, in a flaming bad temper that overwhelmed even the elation that the rain had induced in me. He poured it all out.

The ambassador had given him a little lecture before the meeting, along with one of his medium dry sherries. 'Willie, I've been wanting to have a word with you for some time, for your own good, you know. Nothing very serious. And nothing that can't be corrected. But this is your first posting, and it's important your career gets off to the right start. Now I know how difficult it is to settle into this kind of life at the beginning. It's just that you don't want to start getting the wrong sort of reputation.'

'What sort of reputation is that, sir?' asked Willie with genuine surprise.

'Of bucking the system. Of rocking the boat. You don't seem to accept the embassy's judgment. I've seen that in the various conferences we have. Now I don't ask you to accept my view or that of any other senior member of the embassy as absolute, infallible. And I admire your contributions and suggestions—where these are based on more than conjecture. But please row with the team rather than against it. That also goes for all those off-duty contacts you've been having with local citizens outside official embassy auspices. Please curb them.'

'You've heard about those?'

'Of course. The danger is that you could

end up compromising this embassy if they should continue. Formal embassy channels are quite adequate for the task to hand—of representing Britain's interests in al-Dawah and of conveying accurate information about the state of the country's economy and politics. Now, let's go and see the old boy. And remember what I told you. Please don't give him the impression there are differing views in the embassy.'

Getting in to see Haddad was an experience in itself. The spectacularly dressed guards at the entrance led Willie and the ambassador into an office immediately past the main entrance to the government palace. There a white-clad and impeccably polite man in spectacles asked them to wait, pointing them towards two chairs. They were there nearly forty minutes, with H.E growing visibly more impatient by the moment. The time passed quickly for Willie, as he tried to assess the significance of the ticking off, while still smarting from the ambassador's reproof.

The ambassador eventually exploded: 'Our appointment was for twelve o'clock!' The polite man smiled magnificently and said nothing. 'Could you please tell His Excellency the minister that the British ambassador is waiting.' The man smiled again and nothing happened.

The ambassador tipped himself forward to the edge of the chair, as if preparing to jump. A minion held the door open, and a little man in a white suit and dark tie tripped in. 'Please come this way. His Excellency is so sorry to keep you: pressing affairs of state, you know.' The ambassador smiled as though he did.

They were ushered into a beautifully carpeted, sparsely decorated corridor in the inner palace, which was populated by legions of idle men at desks and guards lounging against walls. The man knocked at a little door and they went into a magnificently upholstered room, with chairs all around. Others were waiting in these chairs.

They were told to sit down again. They did so, fuming. It soon became apparent that the others in the room were people who were also waiting, in strict order of arrival. Anyone had the right to turn up to this great man's office to ask to see him. An appointment apparently counted for nothing. Cups of strong, bitter black coffee were brought to the two Britons.

Willie began to be amused by the

135

ambassador's growing fury. At length he strode up to the table where the male secretaries sat doing nothing in a row. 'Would you tell His Excellency that the British ambassador has been waiting an hour and a half to see him, and that there will be a major diplomatic incident if I have to wait much longer. In five minutes, I will walk through that door.' He pointed. The man read the seriousness in his eyes, and walked to the door nonchalantly as though his masculinity would somehow be impaired if it looked as though he was responding to the ambassador's anger.

Within a couple of minutes they were whisked through. Haddad rose impressively from his desk. A big, stooped man, he was old and slow-moving, but his face was alive and vigorous. He spoke excellent English, was curiously unceremonious and direct, and came straight to the point. 'I am so sorry you were kept waiting. I did not realise it was you. So many people come to see me, and my helpers are so ignorant. One loses track of who is coming.'

'You look very well, Salim,' said H.E, putting on his most ingratiating expression.

'I am so tired. Always so much work. Well?'

'It is a great privilege, Your Excellency, to have the opportunity...' The minister was visibly impatient as H.E made his standard speech about Britain's relations with al-Dawah.

When he had finished, Haddad said, 'These are matters for our trade ministers. What is your assessment of the political situation here?'

H.E was discomfited. 'I think, on the whole, that your country enjoys a reasonable degree of political stability—'

'I think,' said the minister, suppressing a brief, concentrated expression of distaste, 'That we are on the edge of a revolution.'

H.E reddened, caught off balance by the man's directness. 'From what quarter, Your Excellency?'

The big man sighed and flapped his hand nonchalantly. 'The country is being modernised at breakneck speed. Much too fast. The people's traditions are being trampled upon.'

'But the threat from the left is being controlled.'

'The left was never a threat. It could become one only if the traditions of the people are flouted and chaos ensued. A country is like an old man; it can be

137

made to change only slowly. Otherwise it gets angry.'

'So you think that Islam is the most serious problem the government faces?' asked Willie. The ambassador turned a beady eye on him.

'It goes without saying,' said Haddad dismissively.

The ambassador intervened hurriedly. 'Your Excellency, what is your view of the future of Anglo-Dawaian relations over the next five years?'

The minister's eyes glazed across. 'We believe in pursuing the close co-operation and the traditional links that have bound our two countries for centuries—'

Afterwards, in the car, the ambassador said, 'You're not off to a very good start.'

When Willie returned to the flat, I comforted him and gave him a drink. He put an arm round me and we felt closer than we had for ages. And then Willie said, 'I didn't tell you what H.E said about you.' My heart stood still for a moment. Not another attack. 'He said you more than made up for me. You were diligent in your duties, intelligent, and a pleasure to look at and talk to. Funny how a man can be so stupid about so many things and right about just one,' said Willie, sweetly.

In the months to come, though, Willie became morose and restless. He would speak to me less and less, and seemed preoccupied with his work. He grew obsessed with the idea of an Islamic revolution; when he got home, he would drink and rail against the ambassador for his failure to see what was going wrong. He thought of writing a secret despatch directly to the Foreign Office. I told him not to be so silly, he would surely be drummed out of the service.

Curiously enough, my own happiness seemed to be increasing. I was growing more distant from Willie, but my sense of security within the embassy was increasing. I was given a great lift by the ambassador's approval. Suddenly it seemed to me that most people at the embassy looked upon me with approval. They were friendly, and the more I responded, the friendlier they got. I was firm friends now with the Quennells; and even Hugo liked to gossip with me. The junior staff—the secretaries—seemed to enjoy talking to me at the embassy parties held for them. My poor social background and my shyness no longer seemed so much of a handicap. Only Mrs Pugh couldn't stand me, and I began to realise that she was thoroughly unpopular. Colonel Pugh, on the other hand, made passionate attempts to get close to me at parties. I felt tempted at times to respond to his advances, to infuriate Mrs Pugh. But now that I was more content with myself, I felt it would be petty and mean-minded.

The problem lay with Willie, not Mrs Pugh. My social happiness was starting to fill the void left in my personal life. I deliberately shut out of my mind the hope and the memory that I could find fulfilment in my personal life; these things were chosen for you. I thought that as Willie grew more embittered I even detected a sort of envy in him at my growing assurance, a desire to puncture my self-confidence. But what did he want of me? I was no longer the social cripple who held him back. I had tried and tried for him, and was winning through. How else could I satisfy him?

One Friday night we went to the Quennells for a dinner party; it had taken a great deal of persuading to get Willie to go. We had no sooner entered the comfortable drawing room of their modern, well-equipped house than Willie let out a cry: 'Sarah!'

'Willie!' He embraced a girl I had never seen before. She wore distinctly bohemian dress: a long, multicoloured skirt; a loose-fitting top which looked Indian in origin and had a transparency about it that revealed the outline of a bra underneath. She was extraordinarily good-looking, with strong, pale blue eyes under fine pencil eyebrows, a nose that was elegant and pointed without being prominent, finely arched cheekbones and a chin that had prettiness and pertness without being weak. Her long blonde hair cascaded back from where it was held in place, by a ribbon, down to her shoulders.

'This is my wife, Jill,' he said, turning to introduce me. 'This is Sarah Craven. We're very old friends. We've known each other for ages. We used to go to all the smart parties together.' Willie was beaming with pleasure at having made contact with a representative from the home front.

'I had heard that Willie was married,' she said to me. 'He's a hard one to look

141

after, with all his moods. I hope you don't pander to him too much.' She was so at ease, so natural. We all laughed.

'Pander to me? Jill keeps me well trained!' said Willie.

'Was he so impossible even as a boy?' I asked.

'Worse than impossible. He was good-looking, and maddeningly cold and detached. None of us could stand him, although we were all attracted. I don't think anyone ever got him to unwind.'

There was a slightly shocked silence at this. It was a little forward for a diplomatic gathering. 'If I'd known that was all you were after, I'd have jumped on you like a shot,' said Willie.

'Now, now,' said Quennell, laughing. 'You're supposed to make passes in private, after dinner.' We all suddenly became self-conscious, but went off and had a jolly conversation together. She was volubly bouncy and self-confident, totally unlike us diplomats with our stilted, predictable conversation. She was amusing, daring, poking fun at us, and highly intelligent. We were all a little exhausted by her, myself included.

She was a journalist, on assignment

from the American magazine *Time*. She had been one of the lucky ones who had had an opportunity for independence as soon as she left university, and she loved it; she travelled all over the world, visiting countries for a week or two at a time. It was like being a mini-diplomat, with none of the responsibilities, or the boring parties, or being stuck in one place. I envied her like mad. She had us all enthralled by her gossip about the places she had been to.

Quennell watched her sardonically as though he had seen too many journalists. Also present, and sceptical, was McQuarry the resident stringer for a dozen news-papers. He was a dour-faced, humorous man who eyed us all with amusement and, misogynist that he was, couldn't stand her.

She talked without a break through dinner, talked about where she'd been, who she'd met. She talked to Willie about life in London, and what had happened to all their old acquaintances. She asked me and the others about how much we enjoyed life in al-Dawah, and I lied politely, although I could read in her eyes that she considered us as dull as ditchwater. And yet I couldn't help but like her. I suppose that was true of most of us: She had a natural bubbling enthusiasm, a lack of pretension, a directness, an unselfconsciousness that endeared her to people.

At length McQuarry leaned across the table. 'Sarah, why have they sent you down here?' he asked. 'Do they reckon something's up?'

'I'll bet you're interested,' she shot back.

'I've been telling the whole bloody world for years that the place is about to blow up.' He was getting drunk and slurring his speech.

'For fifteen years, in fact,' said Quennell dryly.

'Och, you know me better than that. I said the place was going down the drain ever since I arrived—I wouldn't have stayed otherwise.' He chuckled. 'But it's only in the past six months it's been apparent for all to see.'

'What's gone wrong?' asked the girl, suddenly, with professional interest.

'The economy's in a shambles. They've tried to expand too fast. There's bottlenecks all over the place. It takes two months to get anything unloaded at the ports. They're printing money like mad. Inflation's rising like a bloody rocket.

They've got a trade deficit of hundreds of millions—all for a piddling country like this!' You could see the diplomats visibly shrinking from the old journalist's outspokenness and drunkenness. 'They bankroll themselves by borrowing money from Saudi Arabia next door. It's a shambles. All for this bloody modernisation. Electric cables, pylons, roads, all over the bloody place in a country where nine tenths of the people haven't got electricity or cars.'

'Come on, man,' put in Quennell. 'they'll never have them if they don't put up the electricity grid in the first place.'

'Yes, but you can't do it all at once. It's madness. It's all General al-Ashraf's fault. The man's a power-hungry egomaniac; the poor wee kid of a Sultan's completely taken in by him.'

'You think there'll be a coup?' asked Quennell archly.

McQuarry suddenly retreated into his shell. 'Oh, there's lots of things going on.'

Sarah said. 'It's the communists, isn't it? That's what we've heard. That the rebel forces are closing in and a *putsch* is being prepared by radical officers convinced of the inevitability of defeat. Then al-Dawah will join the Soviet bloc; and Saudi Arabia and it's oil will come under threat. That's what's going on, isn't it?'

McQuarry shrugged. 'I think it's more complicated than that. But you'll see it soon enough, if you do your homework.'

I asked her, to change the subject. 'But what's it really like, being a roving foreign correspondent? Don't you get tired of always being in a different place?'

She put on a look of defensive hardness. 'It's everything I've ever wanted. Really. I love seeing different things, different people, all the time. One never stays long enough in a country to get bored.'

'You get rootless though,' put in McQuarry. 'I did it once. You don't know where you are when you go home, how to relate to people. I was never able to settle down again.'

'It depends on the individual,' Sarah retorted. 'I'm sure I could go back to Britain. But I'd be bored.'

'That's another way of saying what I said,' observed McQuarry dryly.

'But what do you do when you arrive in a place all alone?' put in Lavinia suddenly, in her down-to-earth fashion.

'What I've done here. There's always the embassy circle—they're always glad enough of a new face. And fellow journalists—usually a few more than here. And even the local governments—they want to see you to publicise their achievements. I can arrive in a country, request interviews for the next two days and get them all: something it takes you diplomats all year to do; and you have the disadvantage, also, that you never meet people of different shades of the political spectrum.'

'I expect you get plenty of bedding in, too,' said Willie, with a wild ring in his voice.

'Willie!' I exclaimed, shocked. There was an astounded silence round the table.

She said, hardly less vituperatively. 'Plenty. And it's the most marvellous fun. Different men in different capitals. How sad it must be for you, Willie, in your pinstripe conventionality, stuck in one place. But you're only doing what you always wanted: the right thing socially.' Only then did I glimpse what there must have been between them.

Quennell broke in loudly. 'We had the most extraordinary quantity of rain last weekend. At least two inches. Flooded half the qat plantation. Probably do the local people good...'

I wasn't going to be the first to speak in the car on the way back. Willie puffed furiously at a cigarette, as the driver inched his way into the square in the old city in front of the house. We ascended the steps from the foul-smelling ground floor without speaking, past Hugo Hennessy's apartment, up to our own flat. Willie poured himself a malt whisky—a whole glass of it, I'll swear. I said with utter weariness, 'Don't you think you've had enough?'

'One can never have enough,' he growled angrily.

'Did you love her very much?' I asked quietly.

'Oh, for God's sake don't start,' he said from somewhere within himself. 'I knew her, that's all. She was part of our crowd, our social set. I couldn't stand her then. I can't stand her now. What right has she to come in here from outside to tell us what an interesting life she leads, how boring our lives are?'

'McQuarry was bloody to her.'

'McQuarry was right, he's done it. Can you imagine what it must really be like living out of a suitcase, arriving in a capital full of total strangers, groping your way about, your only refuge a cold hotel room, despairingly ringing people up to make contact with human life? Can you imagine? We're the lucky ones.'

'There was nothing between you?'

'Nothing. I just couldn't stand it any more. She used to lay every man in Oxford. I'm sure she does the same now.' He gulped back more of the whisky. I suddenly felt sorry for him.

'I'm sure you were the one who held out,' I said smilingly, putting a hand to his cheek.

'For God's sake, darling,' he said. But he took it.

His attitude towards me changed completely in the next weeks, and I knew then beyond doubt that he was seeing her. He was kind and attentive. He came back early in the evenings. Instead of his usual distant, difficult, detached self, he was almost charming, and very self-mocking. I allowed myself to be taken in, but even he couldn't have been deceived by my attempts to cover up the hurt and anxiety in my eyes as he kissed me gently in the evenings. I couldn't fight the loneliness that was coming over me, the sudden certainty that a chapter in my life was ending. I imagined she saw him during office hours. Life felt so different now that he had gone with someone else. I felt that I had irreversibly lost a part of him, and therefore of myself.

It was only a fortnight after the dinner party, that Lavinia Quennell asked me to tea at their house. In her firm, gentle way she said, 'Jill, there's something I must tell you.'

'Don't,' I said stiffly. 'I know.'

But she persisted. 'He goes to the hotel at lunchtime. Everyone in the embassy is talking about it. You must know, because it's better to be let down gently now by a friend than by someone else later.' I nodded dully. She paused. 'I'll tell you something—but promise never to repeat it to anyone else. It may help. When I was first married to Peter, after about two years, I found out that he had slept with another woman. She was only a secretary. But I felt devastated. And then when it all broke up—quite discreetly, I assure you—our love became stronger than ever. But you must confront him now. Force him to break it off now.'

'He won't listen to me.'

'Then talk to her.' She was quite insistent. 'Don't make it easy for them, or something serious may grow out of it. Show them you care. It'll make him aware of your feelings, and it'll fight her influence. Don't be so passive,' she said almost angrily, like a schoolmistress, and I felt ashamed of myself. 'Peter's offered to talk to him,' she added.

'No,' I said. 'I'll deal with this myself. I don't want anyone else to interfere. Although,' I added, in case she took offence, 'I'm grateful to you.'

I knew enough about him to know that I would only go to him as a last resort. I could confront him only with an ultimatum. He wouldn't listen to me otherwise. I was prepared to deliver the ultimatum. I had had almost enough. He had behaved monstrously at every turn. And yet—though I couldn't think why—every time I steeled myself I knew I was deeply bound to him, too deeply to get out easily. I hated him because I loved him, because I knew that things would have been so different if that initial openness, that generosity, that shared love we had known in the first few weeks of our marriage had survived.

It had been exposure to the outside world that had changed it; I knew that. Rather like a piece of film, his vision had been overexposed when he realised that he would have to live not just with me but with many others, who represented his social life, his career advancement, his success. He had been afraid I might hold up his success, and for a while I felt he was justified. And then slowly I had come to understand that there were many people like me, shy at first, afraid of the social pressure, who gradually became relaxed as they realised that other people were exactly like them.

But he had not yet come to see that, and I could see the dangers when a flame from his past life, a woman who seemed to represent glamour and success, walked into it. And because I could understand the reason—although I hated him for his weakness—I could not hate him as a person. He bore me no malice; he was a victim of circumstance, of his own failure to understand himself. He would learn, in time; as Lavinia had pointed out, a young husband's restlessness was a common phenomenon.

If only I had understood then that, though one may bear no real malice, a malice born of misunderstanding is just as serious.

It was because I pitied him, because I was convinced that he would change, that I would not let him go, was determined not to let him go. As for me—what had I been, what had I expected of myself throughout our early years of marriage, but to be an extension of him? I would bear his children, I would help his career. His happiness was mine.

I decided to go and see her. I rang her at the Taj Mahal. She was out. I left a message for her to ring me. She didn't. I rang the following day and suggested that she come out for tea one day. She said she was very busy. I said I would meet her wherever she wanted. Eventually she asked if I would come to the hotel that evening for a drink. It was all wrong, diplomatically and socially. As the nonoffended party, she ought to have tried to accommodate me. But journalists are not diplomats. I went along.

She was wearing trousers and a cream canvas shirt. She looked rather defiant, aggressive and edgy. I thought she had been drinking already. She said what I knew, that we could have a drink only in the Omar Khayyam bar. As two unaccompanied women we attracted a lot of looks from the rather shifty-looking men doing drunken deals there; but at least we found seats. We didn't say anything until the drinks arrived. I said 'I came about Willie.' I had expected to be much angrier, but anger is difficult to premeditate.

She said, 'I know. But it isn't my responsibility. I don't have to take your feelings into account.'

'Don't you?' I asked, with genuine surprise. 'I know I would if—if I were tempted. Otherwise they would weigh on me.'

'They don't weigh on me. Obviously, I would prefer it if no one were hurt. But I have feelings too. So does Willie. If he cares for me more than for you, that's the luck of the game. We all look after our own interests.'

'Do you really feel anything for him? Or is he just a bit of fun, something to keep you amused while you're in al-Dawah? There's not much else to do for relaxation.'

She looked as though she were grasping hopefully at what I was saying. 'Well, there's nothing for you to worry about in that case. When I go, Willie'll return to you.'

'That's not a very pleasant thing to say.'

She shrugged. 'I didn't suggest we have a meeting. Some unpleasantness is usually the price of happiness.'

'So you do care for him?'

'I didn't say that,' she said, a little heatedly. 'What is important is that he can do what he wants. If he wants to be with me, and I enjoy his company, that's his choice. I don't have to ask your permission.'

'Have you ever thought about what you're doing to him? About his career. Everyone in the embassy knows.'

'Of course they don't.' She seemed genuinely surprised. 'We've been very discreet.'

'How do you imagine I know? I was told by one of Willie's colleagues. You're ruining him; and you're ruining me. But it means nothing at all to you. You're having your fun, and when you leave you won't see the mess you've left behind.'

I suppose I must have sounded very bitter, because she was bitter back. 'If you can't keep your husband, that's your problem. I know that I could keep mine.'

I got up stiffly. 'Goodbye,' I said formally.

She looked startled. She didn't get up. All she said was, 'If it makes you feel better, I'm not in love with him. And I'll—I'll think about what you say.' She said this with feeling, with sincerity, as though yielding to emotions she had been trying to kick, as though the hard act had all been a front. But I was too angry and confused and bitter to respond, and I just left, blinking back tears.

I heard later from Lavinia that Peter Quennell had seen Willie about it the following day. As Lavinia told it, Peter had put on his most paternal, one-man-of-the-world-to-another act. They had bought drinks at the embassy club and walked over to a corner of the garden where they were alone.

'Look, Willie,' Quennell had said. 'You mustn't mind my speaking frankly about something that ought to be none of my business.'

Willie knew what was coming. 'So it isn't.'

'It's just I can't watch a good man letting himself down and letting others down too. You're ruining yourself by playing around with the girl. She's just a fly-by-night—you know it and I know it. She isn't going to hang around in the dreary diplomatic world. She wants her fun. She's making an ass of you. You've called into question your discretion, your judgment, your loyalty—just about all the qualities that make for a successful career in the service. And you're breaking the heart of that lovely girl, your wife.'

'I'm the best judge of my marital affairs,' Willie said coolly.

'For God's sake man, recognise a bit of friendly advice when you get it! I'm not one of those up there—although they'll get onto you fast enough. I'm trying to help you both.' Quennell had lapsed out of his rather clipped diplomatic tones into a soft Lincolnshire burr.

'Thanks. But I choose my own friends, and I look to them for advice,' said Willie, as cold as steel.

Quennell looked at him disbelievingly and shook his head slowly. 'On your own head be it, man.'

Dawnay put the typescript in his briefcase and locked it. He glanced around the little room, so consoling in its memory of his university days, when you cared about nothing, just about simple possessions: the little wooden desk, the simple bed, the shelves laden with books, the washbasin in the corner. A monastic cell. It was all a thinking man needed. He glanced out of the windows, at where daylight was fading over the little green quad with its two languid trees staining the lawn with their shadows. The outside world, with all of its problems, seemed a long way off. Maybe he should have escaped into the academic life. He picked himself up off the bed and donned smart brown trousers. He didn't put on a tie.

They had met in the same small hotel throughout the affair. It had been his little extravagance, his way of celebrating a considerable pay rise at the office. He had known her a long time: She had been at Oxford with him, although they scarcely knew each other in those days.

One night in London they had met at a mutual friend's party, and he had gone for her. She had said no at the time, because she knew his motive was sexual, and at that age you needed something more. He had got married, she had got married, they hadn't seen each other in years. He had heard she had been divorced.

One day he was in Oxford, to talk to a seminar of English students. He had tracked down her telephone number and called up. When they met again, they were ready to make love. He, because he had always desired her body, that large ample frame with its all-cushioning flesh, the mouth that never quite said no. She because she was lonely and she liked him and sex was no longer the sacred cow that it had been in her youth. They had met occasionally, when he could get away for a weekend, for over a year. And then it had tapered off. There had been no passion in it, just sex for him and companionship for her; they had grown a little tired of seeing too much of each other.

That was eight years before. He had seen her once or twice since then, and absence had rekindled interest. She was obviously pleased to see him when they met and they kissed, not lightly, on the lips. 'You look better than ever,' he said, truthfully.

'So do you,' she lied. She was shocked by the change in his appearance. Whereas once he had been distinguished-looking, if a little too carefully dressed and groomed, now his eyes had sunk back in their sockets, the hair hung loosely on his head, and his skin seemed taut and dry. The old good looks could not be vanquished, but they had retreated. A little colour seemed to return to his cheeks when he caught sight of her. She said, 'It's just like old times.'

He smiled. 'I refuse to give you permission to marry again.'

'Who said I was going to get married again?' she asked, surprised.

'If you should ever want to, you'll have to come and settle scores with me first.' She smiled happily, and he noticed a few cracks of age, at the side of the mouth and under the eyes, that had been expertly concealed.

They made love after dinner. She was very aroused, very active, more so than on previous occasions, enjoying herself in the act. Dawnay felt curiously dispassionate, as she used her hands and mouth to arouse him to the performance he might otherwise have been unable to give—as though his sexuality had nothing to do with his mind, being merely an animal response to animal stimulation.

She sensed it when she tried to arouse him a second time and failed. His mind was elsewhere, in a far-off place twenty-two years earlier, puzzling, puzzling, puzzling, turning over all the evidence as to who it might be. There were only two candidates now. Only two left who could have known as much as the author of the book had known: the ambassador and Peter Quennell.

'What is it?' She breathed the words softly into his ear. He turned and glanced at her; she wasn't angry, just concerned. He trusted her. He poured it all out. She just ruffled the short, greying hairs on his chest as she listened.

'Blackmail must be the most horrible thing,' she said. 'Especially if you haven't done anything to be blackmailed about.'

'I haven't,' he said, with a touch of pique.

'That's what I said,' she said gently. 'Or you don't know why he's doing it. It can't be for money, or you would have heard from him by now.'

'That's my view too. But if not, what is he doing it for?'

'I think it's Quennell. From what you've told me. I think he hated you for class reasons. And because of the way he thinks you treated Jill.'

'He's not the type. Too dull, too unimaginative. Can you imagine him writing a book like that? And what for anyway? Old Grantley's more the type: sensitive, fence-sitting, aloof. He could write like that.'

'It's all very interesting. The old school-tie-stuffed-shirt diplomat and the grammar school commercial attaché. Who did the deadly deed?'

Suddenly he felt an overpowering urge to be alone. She was interested in the problem because it was a distraction from her routine life. She was more interested in the idea than concerned about him. He mustn't be surprised at that, or feel sorry for himself. It was just that he mustn't burden others with his problems, or rely on their help to sort them out. He looked at the body beside him, and he felt no stirring within. It was as if the sex they had had was a physical need, now sated. He made his excuses, observed the disappointment in her face, dressed and left.

When it came to the point, he hadn't the nerve to see Grantley. The man had been his boss, overpowering, imposing, disapproving for eighteen months, during a traumatic period of his life. To go and accuse him of being a blackmailer required courage of an order Dawnay would do anything to avoid having to summon up. He went to see Quennell instead.

Quennell took some finding. Since leaving the diplomatic service at the age of forty-five, he had held a number of posts with different companies, and two or three of them were reluctant to provide details. At length, after much telephoning from his All Souls room, Dawnay found that Quennell was now working with a company called Translucent Optics. He rang the company and was connected to a secretary, who was downright discourteous.

'Can you tell me what it's about?'

'Just give him my name. He'll talk to me. We were old colleagues together.'

'Mr Quennell is very busy. He may be in a conference right now.'

'Just tell him.'

She came back to him a few moments later. 'I wonder if you could tell me what it's about.'

Dawnay felt the urge to throw the receiver to the floor. 'It's about my wife. Jill. Tell him that.'

Quennell came to the phone. His voice was quiet, clipped, to the point, a man accustomed to saying no more than he needed. Dawnay recognised the slight Lincolnshire burr through it all; if anything, it had become more pronounced, because he had dropped the foreign office twang he previously affected. 'Willie, I'm glad to hear from you after all these years. What can I do for you?'

'Can you meet me for a drink? Anytime that suits you.'

'Well, I'm very tied up at the moment. Very tied up. Can't we talk on the phone?'

'No,' said Dawnay emphatically. 'And it's urgent. I think you know what it's about.'

Quennell hesitated. 'Can you come to my office at about six o'clock? I can give you a drink here. We can talk in private.'

Dawnay agreed. It seemed the best he would get.

An hour and a half later, he was back in London, crossing the Thames to the concrete-and-glass structure that now contained Peter Quennell. He had difficulty parking the car. He felt very small as he walked to the sleek main lobby of the building; he was made to wait, leafing through some unamusing magazines in a polished leather chair for a while, until someone came to escort him upstairs.

They rode in a steel lift to a floor high up in the building and were ushered along deeply carpeted corridors. He was shown into a room containing a long table and magazines about business efficiency; he stood there admiring the desolate view of South London tower blocks for a full twenty minutes until Quennell came in with a practiced smile and an outstretched hand. 'Come in, come in,' he said expansively. 'It's been a long time.'

Quennell had changed altogether. In place of the awkward, sometimes wryly humorous, sometimes taciturn, usually self-conscious middle-aged diplomat was a man of accomplished professional poise and a face as friendly and impersonal as that of a clock measuring the time he spent with his visitors. It was all surface, of course. Dawnay knew the real chip-on-the-shoulder man underneath. 'What'll you have?' asked Quennell, gesturing towards a well-stocked cabinet.

'Gin and tonic.'

'I'll join you.' He filled two glasses and motioned Dawnay to a sofa in the corner, where they settled comfortably. 'This really is a surprise.' Dawnay noted with irony the executive language that Quennell had unconsciously adopted. He took in the impeccable suit, the stiff clean collar, the perfect, bland, faintly hard expression of the businessman before him.

Quennell said, 'Well, and how have you been keeping yourself since you left the service?'

'You know,' said Dawnay pointedly. 'In publishing.'

'Still in publishing. Yes, I remember you had gone into that.' He took a sip from his glass. 'You know, I envy you for going into something like that. It's probably not as well paid as this. But it must be a damned sight more interesting.'

'I'm sure you find your job interesting.' Dawnay couldn't conceal the trace of contempt he felt for a man who had found his niche in the plodding, uniform world of industry. 'How's Lavinia?'

'Well. Very well. We had our first grandchild eight months ago. Both our girls are happily married. What more could one want in life?'

'What indeed?' said Dawnay.

Quennell made a slight gesture of impatience with his hand, while the smile stayed rooted to his face.

'All right, I'll get to the point,' said Dawnay nervously. 'It's about the book. The book I've been sent about Jill.' He paused pregnantly.

'The book about Jill. Go on,' said Quennell carefully.

'You sent it, didn't you?'

Quennell said, politely, 'I haven't the faintest idea what you're talking about, Willie. But go on.'

Dawnay's nervousness exploded into rage. 'Of course you have! You loathed me in al-Dawah—always have. I don't know why; and I can't think why you've decided to open the bloody closet after all this time—' he was on the edge of his seat, trembling with anger.

Quennell's eyes registered alarm for a

moment. He recovered quickly. 'Calm down, man, calm down,' he said, leaning forward again. 'Don't get so upset.' He put hand on Dawnay's knee, and Dawnay instinctively shrank away. 'Tell me what's worrying you.'

Dawnay told him about the book, nervously, with a pained expression in his eyes.

'And you think it's me bothering you? Why?' asked Quennell with genuine interest.

'Because we hate each other. Always have.'

'Correction,' the businessman thoughtfully said. 'You hate me. I pity you. You hate me because you don't know how to cope with the challenge of someone far beyond your social milieu. You don't believe I'm up to your standards, whatever they may be, and yet you're afraid I exceed them. I pity you because you care about such things. I'm damn sure I don't. I just care about doing a job as best I can, leading a simple life, having a wife and family that I love. I pity you all the more because of the responsibility you bear for depriving yourself of the only woman who could have given you happiness; one of

168

the most worthwhile human beings I have ever met.'

'So it was you,' said Dawnay, his eyes glittering dangerously.

Quennell looked at him levelly and shook his head. 'The guilt you bear, and will have to bear all your life, is a far worse punishment than anything I could do. I pity you for that most of all. As for the book, I suggest you throw it away or go to the police. Solve the problem like a man. Put it out of your mind or do something about it beyond making a fool of yourself in front of people you haven't seen in more than twenty years.'

Quennell's words stang. Dawnay was suddenly conscious of his own moth-eaten and frayed suit, of his unkempt thinning hair, of the appearance he presented in front of this sleek representative of the new ruling class. His eyes brimmed with tears, drowning his anger. His glass suddenly slipped from his hands, waking him up. He picked it up. His trouser legs felt clammy. 'I'm sorry,' he mumbled.

'I'll get you another, stiffer one. Knock it back. And then get out of here,' said Quennell. Yet the hardness had gone out of his voice.

Dawnay looked up. 'No thanks. I must go.'

Quennell put a hand on Dawnay's shoulder, and looked him in the eye. 'Do yourself a favour. Drop this whole thing. Burn the book or throw it in the Thames. You'll forget all about it.'

Dawnay said coldly, 'I can't imagine what satisfaction you get out of working here, insulated from the world in this ghastly building.' It was like the conversation about Jill all over again. They looked at each other for a minute; then the publisher, recovering his dignity, left without a word. Quennell shrugged, and drained his glass.

It was dark when he got home. He felt tired and ill. He realised he hadn't eaten all day. His legs felt tired and all his muscles ached and he felt strangely light-headed, even though he hadn't drunk anything. He went straight upstairs to the bathroom. When he emerged, Sarah was standing at the bottom of the stairs, a look of exasperation on her face.

He didn't know why she was looking at him like that. He said, 'God, I need a drink. And something to eat.'

'You can make them yourself,' she said tersely.

'For God's sake, darling, I'm dead tired.' He looked at her. 'Please.'

'Where were you last night?'

'I had to stay up in Oxford to discuss the project. For God's sake, I don't have to make excuses like a six-year-old,' he said irritably.

'And I don't have to obey your orders like one. The Marshams came yesterday for drinks.'

'I hope you made my excuses. Crashing bores, all of them.' She suddenly left where she had been standing, and strode into the drawing room, slamming the door behind her.

He didn't care. He went to the kitchen and found, among a cluster of bottles, one of Scotch; he helped himself liberally, without adding water. Then he found some biscuits and spread a cheese pâté over them. He heard her stomp upstairs and shut the door of the bedroom. He felt relaxed. He was too tired now to think. Clutching his glass he made his way to the sitting room, to the most comfortable chair, and sank into an exhausted, deep sleep.

FOUR

July 14. That was when it began. I could hardly be expected to forget it, because I witnessed it personally.

The day was characteristically like a blasting furnace. I was returning from a lunchtime drink with the consul's wife, who I got on with. She lived in the new town, but the old town was not far from her house, within walking distance. I was walking slowly, happily along, oblivious to the usual stares from the men, past the tatty row of shop fronts along the road that led from the new city to the old. Battered, tinny American and German cars clattered by on the rough surface, sending up clouds of dust that irritated one's eyes.

I was admiring, as one had to every time, the spectacle of the cluster of tall buildings that made up the old town, with their familiar black-and-white chocolate-cake appearance. I barely noticed the knots of people standing about, though their presence was unusual for four o'clock in the afternoon, before it became cool enough for people to take their evening stroll and gossip. I had just about reached where the road dipped down into the dusty, urine-smelling bowl where the moat had once run around the old city while the track climbed up to the gate when I became aware of the angry stares all round. They were no longer the curious gazes of men who, recognising that I was a foreign woman with different customs, usually dropped their eyes and hurried past sheepishly. They were fixed, angry, furious looks. The men didn't move, they just stared.

I felt myself hurrying a little, in spite of myself, as in the early days when we had first arrived and I had feared to go out on my own. I climbed the incline to the gate, passed under the central arch and continued down familiar streets that were now littered with broken glass and burning piles of rubble. I could not understand what was happening. I knew it was threatening, dangerous.

There were fewer bystanders here, but women gazed at me, with ill-concealed hostility. A large woman enshrouded by a black shawl and a parrot's beak mask suddenly started screaming at me hysterically from a doorway. I hurried past, looking fixedly ahead, and she didn't follow. I was frightened now.

Then I saw something which nearly froze me with horror. It was a human arm, lying in the middle of the dust; it had a dried, crimson stump. My eyes would not move from the spectacle, my heart was thumping loudly. I thought I was going to be sick. I tore my eyes away and walked on—something told me not to run. I knew now that the streets held real, unknown terrors. I must get back home—quickly.

The hands came at me without warning from all sides. Two grabbed me under each arm, one wrapped itself around my stomach, tugging me back. I had no thought in my mind but one: that my limbs too might be scattered around the streets of this place, for the dogs to gnaw. The arms were strong and forced me back into the recesses of a foul-smelling ground floor. I was pinned against a wall. I forced myself to turn to look into the eyes of my assailants. The men wore the British-style uniforms and the Arab headdresses of the military police.

Unbelievable relief surged up my stomach,

my legs, causing them almost to buckle. The men spoke no English, but they barked at each other and at me and I shook my head slowly, uncomprehendingly. One man, who appeared to be more senior than the rest, a young man with a sly face and uncertain eyes, shouted at me. I at last had the presence of mind to fish my official pass out of my shirt pocket. I showed it to him: His expression changed to one of uncertainty and diffidence. He sought to be deferential. But I could tell he was just as angry and frightened as I was.

There were three men with him. They hustled me gently up some stairs and we found ourselves in a bare, sparsely furnished room. I had regained a little of my self-confidence. I was angry with them for treating me so roughly. I shouted at them in English, but they didn't understand, and it made their commander jumpier and more nervous still. He took my arm, and my fury increased. I was afraid that he might be some sort of renegade, that I might be violated or worse.

He took me over to the window and pointed down the dusty, empty street. I was aware, through my fright and anger, of the sounds and chanting and of surging crowds in the cracking heat. But it was only when the first rioters turned the corner that the explanation of it all began to dawn upon me, and I understood what that bloodied arm had meant and why the soldiers had pulled me to safety inside the building.

The air shimmered so that the marching men seemed like a mirage in the distance, distorted through a curious sort of haze. There were thousands of them, in Arab dress, brandishing sticks and waving fists, chanting furiously in angry rattle-Arabic that seemed to come from their inner chests, like machine-guns. Through the dust above their heads, I saw what I thought must be a sack of rags being tossed up and down, up and down, in rhythmic obedience to their chants. As it approached I realised it was not rags, but a man. I assumed it was their leader, being carried shoulder-high to victory. And then a part of the man came off, a part which it took my horrified senses an instant to realise was a leg; and as the man was tossed up and down, up and down, I saw the rest coming apart—the other leg, then each arm, until there was just the torso and the head, and then that disappeared into the crowd, swallowed into its midst.

With mounting horror I saw a man—a merchant of some sort, because he was fleeing a shop—being seized by rabid men; he was screaming hysterically; he disappeared for a moment into their midst, and then the crowd had another plaything bouncing up and down, up and down above their shoulders.

I pulled away from the window, fighting to control my nausea. The eyes of the commander said everything. I could not believe that the streets I had come to think of over the past few months as utterly peaceful and safe, usually so empty save for playing children and busy women and the odd flock of sheep, could have become the scene of such horror.

Two of the soldiers were covering the staircase with their guns. We all knew it was quite useless. Bullets could not have stopped that crowd, that raging, frenzied torrent of humanity. If they knew we were in the building they would pour up the stairs. They would know: Everyone knew everything that happened in the old city. The crowd would be told. I glanced at the taut, tense faces of the four men, and I could feel there was no safety there. Each one of them, like me, could picture himself as a bundle of rags above the heads of the crowd being torn slowly apart by pulling, tossing hands disintegrating.

The crackle of gunfire we then heard sounded very feeble against the bloodlust pouring from the throats of the crowd. We all turned to peer out of the window. The commander pointed excitedly. There was a line of soldiers about a hundred yards away, kneeling, guns to their shoulders. They were impeccably uniformed and the sight of that disciplined line of men suddenly put new heart into me. I looked at the crowd. No one, it seemed, had been hurt; the soldiers must have been firing over their heads. The crowd wavered only an instant, and then started surging towards the soldiers in a huge uncontrolled mass, hysterical shouts mingling with the war chants. The next crackle of gunfire was barely audible in the maelstrom, yet I was aware that some of those at the head of the crowd had fallen and been trampled underfoot. Still they came on, and the crackle sounded again, fainter still, and some more fell. Sticks and bricks and stones were lobbed in the air as the mad, unstoppable stampede came on down the street.

Another crackle, and I noticed that the crowd was slowing. When they were just three hundred yards away from the troops the crackle sounded again. The soldiers never budged from their position. The ones at the front were staring death in the face. Any hesitation by the marksmen would have been fatal. The press of the crowd would have otherwise forced those at the front forwards, to overwhelm the guns.

This time I could see the little puffs of smoke at the end of the gunbarrels and the men falling not a hundred yards from the building we were in and the screams and confusion as those at the front began to run back, colliding with those at the rear. Then, like a tide turning, the crowd began to accelerate in the same direction. The commander in the room with me barked orders at his men, and they moved to the window, their guns pointing. The volleys below had been so faint that I was not prepared for the volume of the guns' explosion in the room, and I shrank back to the wall as the firing went on for a minute or two. The commander shouted hoarsely at his men; they ran downstairs, and I followed. They had forgotten me. I watched them running to join the serried ranks of troops slowly pushing forward, in the wake of the crowd.

I saw a face I knew—Sarah's. She was flushed with excitement, drunk on the scene, as were two others, including McQuarry, who were with her. 'My God, what are you doing here?' she yelled. I told them. 'You were in the building, you saw what happened?' I told them. 'Thanks,' she said gratefully. The journalists continued in slow pursuit of the moving band of soldiers. I watched her and her little group of newsmen drenched in sweat and dust move on, and I felt grateful to her for having restored me to contact with the world outside, the civilised world outside, before, dazed, I made my way back to the flat.

'Seventy-three dead,' said Willie. 'It's unbelievable. Many thousands injured.' He sank back exhausted into an armchair, reaching for his glass. He rarely smoked, but now he puffed a cigarette nervously without inhaling. The bags under his eyes were hung with weariness. I looked at him with concern. I had almost forgotten my experience of earlier that day. I had been desperately worried when Willie hadn't returned at his usual time of 7:30 PM, and had gone down to Hennessy's flat to see if he, at least, was back. He wasn't. By ten o'clock I felt isolated and terrified in the old city. Perhaps Willie had been caught in the riot. What if he couldn't get through to me?

And then there he was, his usual self-absorbed self, with barely a word of worry or concern for me, complaining of his busy day sorting out the arrangements for the evacuation of British subjects and for the repatriation of property held by Britain, and dealing with enquiries about how to get money out of the country for al-Dawaians, as well as concocting a despatch about the rioting for the Foreign Office. I told him what I had seen and gave him a long description of my adventure.

He was more interested in the details of the rioting than in my safety. 'It's the fundamentalists. Just as I always thought it would be. The pace of al-Ashraf's modernisation programme was too fast for the country. The people hated it: just as I always said, just as McQuarry said, just as the Sultan feared. And that damn fool of an ambassador couldn't be made to see sense! Nor could bloody old Pugh, or even Hennessy. They all thought the army was going to take over. The army's the most hated institution in the land. After today, with all the killings, its anyone's guess what'll happen. They could all slink back to their homes, or there could be full-scale war in the streets. I've asked Hugo to come up the moment he gets back.'

I was desperately tired, but I wasn't annoyed. The more embassy people there were around me the better. I felt a craving for company after the day's events, and a craving for more than just Willie.

Hugo arrived at about half past eleven. It was the first time I had seen him tieless, his hair ruffled, his handsome, impeccable features weary, his eyes sparkling with determination. He and Willie talked over the whole thing interminably. 'The riot could be just a one-off affair, or the whole country could be on the brink of catastrophe,' mused Willie reflectively.

'The situation,' said Hennessy tersely, 'is a lot worse than it seems. The mob is more or less leaderless. It could tie the army down in the capital. The chances of an all-out push by the National Liberation Front, to take advantage of the disunity in the capital, are growing every day. If they succeed, this country could become a Soviet satellite and a pistol pointed at Saudi Arabia's head. Just imagine if the most populous country in the Arabian peninsula falls into Soviet hands!'

I only half-listened. I said at length, 'Well, I'm going to bed to prepare for the day ahead.'

Hugo rose gallantly to his feet. 'Thank you so much Jill. You'll both be coming back tomorrow, joining the evacuation party, I imagine?'

The thought had not occurred to me. 'Why, do you think we should move?'

He looked astonished. 'Of course. I'm getting out as early as I can. I've arranged for the embassy truck to pick all our luggage up. I'm leaving the furniture and just praying that something's left when I get back. If I get back.'

'You don't think we're safe here?' I asked.

He laughed harshly. 'Safe? You've seen it for yourself. The old town's the centre of Islamic militancy. It was down al-Basheh Street today. It could as easily have been down here in the western quarter in al-Qasrah Street itself. We're non-Moslems, infidels. When a mob goes mad, anyone is fair game.'

I could see he was right. I looked at Willie. He said slowly, 'Well, I'm damned if I'm going to run away. I'm going to stay here to observe what happens. Someone in the embassy has to.'

Hennessy looked at him intently. 'Of course you're not staying here. It's bloody suicide.'

'Really?' said Willie, contemplatively.

'Jill, for God's sake, make him see some sense!' said Hugh. It was the first time I had seen his unflappability waver.

I said to Willie coolly. 'I'm not staying here. I'm going with Hugo tomorrow. What you do with yourself is your business.'

Willie looked at me furiously, but I didn't care. He repeated, 'I'm staying. I've got a job to do and it's to report back what's bloody well happening on the ground. And I'll do it.'

Hugo looked at him levelly. 'You're leaving with us tomorrow. That's a direct order from the senior embassy officer on the spot. I don't want to do this, but I'm damned if I'll see a young man like you commit suicide.'

'How do you enforce it?' asked Willie laconically.

'Damn it man, I can ruin your career forever!' exploded Hennessy.

'I can ruin you,' said Willie with disdain; Hennessy flushed deeply. 'Besides, my career may not be the only thing I care about.'

Hennessy gave Willie a long, hard look. 'So be it,' he said tartly. He turned to me. 'Jill, the truck is coming round at seven-thirty promptly tomorrow.' I thanked him. He left to get a few hours sleep.

Willie turned to me after he had gone. 'Running out on me?' he said, more questioningly than angrily.

'What on earth are you staying for?' I asked, completely baffled by what had just happened.

'I care about doing my job properly.'

My tension subsided and I understood him better. He looked at me defiantly, and the defiance blended into uncertainty and for the first time in months he came over spontaneously, of his own free will, to kiss me and to hold me.

My resistance dissolved; I had so long

been denied affection from him that to get it was unbelievable, like a new dawn. He said 'I must. But I'm glad you're going. There's no reason for your life to be endangered.'

The drive the following morning was slow and nerve-racking. It took ten minutes on a normal day. Now it took an hour and a half. Hennessy had managed, with great difficulty, to get a military escort. The army had claimed that all its troops were committed to patrolling the area and that there were none to spare.

We set off, with one army jeep in front, in the embassy truck—which was really a converted Volkswagen, with as much of our personal effects as we could fit in. The streets were utterly deserted and rubble lay strewn around them like discarded children's toys. I could not help gazing out of the windows and was somehow hardened enough by now to gaze without horror—without feeling sick—at the sight of bodies without limbs and a head standing upright on its severed neck, covered in flies, in a doorway, as though placed there deliberately.

We had been moving only ten minutes

through streets barely wide enough for a car, when we rounded a corner and saw the barrier not a hundred yards away. There couldn't have been many behind it, twenty people perhaps. But the shower of bricks and stones and bottles was immediate and lethal. The driver jammed the van into reverse and I could clearly see the wild-staring, angry faces chasing after us. We pulled into a narrow alley that I considered totally impassable, drove fast between two walls that scraped the sides of the car. The engine roar soon drowned out the sound of the crowd.

At length we emerged into a wider street that I recognised, and drove out of the north gate, towards safety. I was expecting an army presence at the north gate, an obvious place for demonstrations. There was a barricade manned by four or five people across the street. A body lay twenty yards in front of it, to the left. Three dogs chewed idly at it. The men at the barricade caught sight of us, and I saw that they were armed with primitive tribal rifles.

The escort car in front of us suddenly accelerated towards them, and I glanced at our driver, who took on a set expression and put his foot down. The car surged forward with a jolt. 'Get down!' barked Hennessy as I watched, mesmerised. I ducked down in the seat. I heard a number of rifle cracks, and the sound of throbbing, strong engines close to me at the bottom of the truck. I braced myself.

The driver broke out in a girlish, hysterical chatter, his grin as wide as his face. We were through unscathed. It still took fifteen minutes from there to the embassy.

The small hallway was in a state of pandemonium. The staff had brought their children in, and they were standing anxiously by. We all anxiously searched each other's face for consolation. My first concern for Willie had been replaced by a blazing anger. That stubborn, wilful, horrible beast! He always did what he wanted, and nothing, not even concern for his career, or his wife, or his life, would stop him.

Peter Quennell came up. 'Thank God you're safe,' he said. 'Where's Willie?' I told him. 'The bloody fool,' was all he said and moved on.

H.E invited a group of the senior

embassy staff into his study, to detach them from the crowd that thronged the little hallway and waiting room. I was asked in, in Willie's absence. H.E's puffed cheeks were flushed, his eyes gazed far off; his expression was grimly set with responsibility. For once he possessed an authority which his genial, distant, bumbling nature had always seemed to lack. He moved his hands continually as he spoke, wiping them on his trousers.

'I've made arrangements for an aircraft to embark British personnel at 11:30 AM on Wednesday. I'm afraid we'll have to grin and bear it until then. We have to get an RAF transport in to take us out, and none will land until the airport is properly secured by government troops. I'm afraid the rioting has extended to the airport area and although the authorities say the situation there is under control, I must be satisfied that that is indeed the case before I can recommend a landing—and before I can risk all your lives taking you to the airport. I propose that the whole embassy, without exception, be on that aircraft.'

There was a stunned silence. It was Peter Quennell who spoke first, anxiously, quietly: 'Sir, are things really that serious?'

'I'm afraid so,' said the ambassador, just as quietly. 'The National Liberation Front broke through at Djebel this morning. I'm told they've covered eighty miles in two hours, because there's nothing to stop them. The army has some defensive positions around the capital, which could hold them up for a day or so. But the army is demoralised. Several units from the front have been flown in to keep order here, which is why the southern front has broken. Salim Haddad informs me that the rioting is expected to continue, as they cannot spare more troops from the front. He has also informed me that the government can no longer spare the troops to protect the embassy. That is the reason I am ordering the evacuation.'

'What the hell's going on?' asked Hennessy distinctly into my ear, as the meeting began to break up. He pulled me forward, to where the ambassador was standing. 'Sir, could we have a quick chat?'

H.E looked distantly at him. 'Of course, Hennessy. But it'll have to be quick.' I noticed that both Quennell and Pugh had moved closer in. There was a look of apprehension in H.E's eyes. 'Why don't

190

you all stay.' The others were slowly filing out of the room. 'Sit down, for God's sake,' said the ambassador wearily.

Hugo said, 'Jim, just what is happening. You've told us nothing.'

H.E was very defensive. 'I've told you all there is to tell.'

'Why isn't Haddad protecting us?'

I could see the dangerous glint in the ambassador's eyes. 'Because we won't come to his rescue.'

'His rescue?' asked Quennell in puzzlement.

'He has sought international support in the government's hour of crisis. The Americans say they would provide a force if it could be joined by contingents from France and Britain, making it multinational. Otherwise the Americans fear they'll be out on a limb, and be denounced as neocolonialists. The British government has declined to join the force, although the French are willing.'

'On what grounds?' asked Quennell quietly.

'I informed them,' said the ambassador, his colour rising, 'that I felt an outside intervention would be unlikely to succeed. That it would inflame the passions of the mob, who are against modernisation, against the secular state, and against the West. I believe that, provided foreign intervention does not take place, this is one of those things that will settle down. Mr Haddad disagreed.'

'Have the French and the Americans now refused to intervene?'

'Yes,' said the ambassador tersely.

'So al-Dawah will be allowed to fall without a murmur,' said Quennell, very quietly.

'I beg your pardon?' said the ambassador stiffly.

'Where the bloody hell's the political attaché?' asked Quennell tersely.

'Willie's still in the old city, observing the fighting,' I said dully. No one said anything for a moment. They all avoided my eye.

The ambassador said dryly, 'I hope he gets back in time to catch the aircraft.'

Quennell interrupted: 'Is there any precedent, sir, for an embassy withdrawing in this way, lock, stock and barrel, leaving not a single person behind?'

'Many,' said the ambassador dryly. 'Wherever our safety is not guaranteed by the local government. That is precedent and reason enough.'

'Is there any precedent,' asked Hennessy, in tones of controlled anger, 'for a country to be delivered into the hands of our enemies because we, the British government are not prepared to help our allies, the United States and France, in assisting its legitimate government? And is there any precedent for an embassy ever having got the analysis of the local situation so hopelessly wrong?'

The ambassador rose, with some dignity. 'I don't think you can have expected an answer to that, Hugo,' he said. 'What chiefly concerns me now is the safety of our people. And I think we have done all that we can to ensure that.' We were being dismissed. We left without another word.

I caught Hugo's arm. 'Please,' I said, 'I've got to bring him in.'

His cold eyes melted slightly. 'I'll work something out. Don't worry.' He walked on; he was clearly still seething from the exchange. I couldn't have cared less. I could think of nothing but Willie and how I hated him, and how I had to get him back. That stubborn, horrible, selfish man. But he was in danger, and I had a duty to him. I hated him, God help me, I hated him. But as I sat in the frightful embassy waiting room, getting angrier and angrier at the embassy's inability to do anything, at the crowd, at the stupid way the evacuation was being organised, I suddenly decided to do something on my own.

I went down the main steps to the little courtyard. Three of the embassy cars were there. I went over to where the drivers stood by uncertainly. I looked towards the gate, where there were men shouting and clamouring to get in, people who claimed some contact with Britain. I turned to Rashid, the driver who had usually worked for us, who was always very deferential to me.

I said, 'We have to go back to the flat, to pick up my husband.' He looked at me, and there was fear in his eyes. I said, with total determination, 'We have to,' and climbed into the car. He shrugged and climbed in. We turned into the narrow forecourt and I shouted at the attendants at the gate, and they let us through.

There were few people and fewer cars about as we drove back. My fear had been conquered by my determination to bring him in, to ensure that, whatever happened, no one would say I had abandoned him. I hated him and I adored him. Hated him for the selfishness that kept him in his front-line position. Adored him for his refusal to run, like all the rest of them in the embassy, Hugo and Peter included.

Nothing untoward happened on the way back. The demonstrators must have been taking a siesta. When we reached the square in front of the apartment, I told the driver to wait and rushed into the house and upstairs. I was ready to lose my temper, viciously, to get him out. When I reached the sitting room, the door was open. I found him there, defeated, demoralised, dejected, crumpled in an old armchair.

He glanced at me as I came in. His eyes lit up momentarily. He said, 'I thought you'd gone.'

'I had. I've come back. I know why you stayed.'

'You know. And yet you came back,' he said slowly.

I nodded. 'I have a duty to you. You can't look after yourself. You are destroying yourself, gradually, by inches. There's still time. Please come with me.'

We were arguing reasonably. There was

no emotion now; we were drained of it. He said, 'I can't. It's no use. I don't love you, Jill. I don't think I ever did, beyond that first fantasy life and the physical attraction. You and I are as different as chalk and cheese. We have different interests, different passions. I love Sarah. She's like me. We think on the same level.'

'She's going to use you, and when she's finished she's going to discard you.'

'No. You don't understand. She loves me, passionately. She wants me to give all this madness up. It's me who's fighting, who's resisting. I can't fight much longer, Jill, I love her and I don't love you, it's as simple as that.'

'And in the same breath you denounce the stupidity of infatuation! Willie, love needs passion on both sides to live. I care passionately for you—in spite of the way you've behaved. I always will, I can't help it. That's the love that endures. One day you'll get fed up with your infatuation, and there'll be nothing. She won't be waiting for you.'

'I tell you it's she that loves me!' His anger had boiled over. He controlled it. I marvelled at my own calm. But then I was fighting for my life.

He went on: 'It's no use. You'd better get back while you still can.'

'I'm staying one night,' I said. 'If you haven't changed your mind by the morning, then I'll leave. Where is she now?'

'She's out, talking to people, covering "the story", as she calls it. For God's sake go before she gets back,' he pleaded.

'No,' I said gently. 'This is my flat, not hers. Don't worry, I won't be in in your way. Just allow me to sleep in my own bed. You can do what you like in here, or in the other room.' I turned away, and went into the bedroom, and lay on the bed, and was left alone with my thoughts. I lay there for four hours, thinking and remembering and feeling.

I know now what was going on during those four hours. She wrote it up in her classic despatches for *Time*. While the mob rioted with unabated savagery, army units kept watch. The Sultan was in perpetual conference with Haddad and General al-Ashraf. They wrangled incessantly, the general urging that the mob be gunned down, Haddad urging the government to promulgate a new Islamic code, to fire al-Ashraf and to drop the modernisation plan that had caused the upheaval. When the Sultan heard the news that outside help from the West would not after all be forthcoming, he dithered and did nothing.

The mob grew in size. An armed force under General al-Qurraishi, al-Ashraf's deputy, set out to reinforce the troops stationed in the old city. It never got there. Instead, General al-Qurraishi crossed the city and marched on the royal palace, where the country's three top men were still conferring. The troops guarding the palace took sides with the superior force. The mutineers broke into the palace, butchered the Sultan, General al-Ashraf, Haddad and most of the cabinet. All the members of the royal family and its retinue who could be found were killed.

The rebels tied the bodies of the Sultan and Haddad to the back of a jeep. What was left of them after the drive to the old city was pulled apart by the crowd. General al-Qurraishi announced that he would set up an Islamic military dictatorship. That night the crowd rampaged wildly through the city, fraternising with the soldiers; guns were fired with wild abandon everywhere, fires lit up the night sky. I did not know what was happening, although I could guess. I lay on my bed, fear having been chased away by misery.

You didn't know, Willie, how deep the misery went, when she came back and I heard your movements together in the room upstairs. You didn't know what every creak of the bed did to me, and how it preyed on my mind that the man I loved, my whole life, was being destroyed. How the memories and hopes of only a year before, which used to brighten the room I was in—our bedroom—had flown by, leaving nothing but black despair. How I had struggled to fit into the social circle you liked, to talk to the people you admired, people who looked down on me because I was not as stupid as they were, or as well born.

It was a sacrifice made in vain because the more accepted I became, the more you seemed to hate me, hate me as though I was tying you to a life you had craved desperately before, and now hated.

You never knew what you really wanted, did you, Willie? You wanted to get ahead and then you grew sick of it all and wanted something new. You could not be satisfied. I occupied a smaller and smaller part of your being, as you strove for change. When she arrived on the scene, she held out the prospect of something new, something different. You seized it.

You had one more chance that night, one more chance to come back, to be satisfied, to scale down, to make an effort at loving me. It would have made it easier for you, because I know you are not a happy man as you read this now in your little box of an office, leading a dull, screwed-down life, no longer travelling. You would have enjoyed yourself more if you had stayed in the diplomatic service and you hadn't been trying so damn hard to get ahead. Where to?

Dawnay flung the typescript down on the table. It bore smudges where he had been holding it too tightly. He couldn't read on. He felt hot and sticky and a vice-like pain had gone through his chest, up his neck.

The office was empty now; his secretary had gone home. The light from the Anglepoise lamp splattered emptily on the desk where the typescript had been.

He couldn't go on. It hurt too much, and he was afraid of the ending. The room's dimensions seemed to have widened when he got up. It seemed rather frighteningly large. His faculties seemed sharper: He could hear every rustle in the building and the sound of the traffic outside, magnified. He picked up the telephone slowly and surely, and dialled a number he had once been too afraid to dial.

The voice on the other end sounded shrunken. It has lost its deep timbre. The writer had to be him because there was no one else. Sir James Grantley, K.C.M.G, was in his last year as Chairman of Greenfield Park, a magnificent eighteenth-century conference centre run by retired senior diplomats, which hosted foreign discussion groups and delegations. When Dawnay told Grantley he wanted a meeting, he was invited down. Just as Dawnay knew he would be. Grantley sounded quiet and thoughtful at the other end, as though he had been expecting the call.

The drive to Greenfield was relatively traffic-free at that time of night. But the way Dawnay felt made it seem endless. His hands on the driving wheel felt disembodied, not a part of him, and he sometimes wondered whether he was genuinely in control of the vehicle. He was utterly without passion, as though he couldn't care less if the car did suddenly swerve across the road into an oncoming vehicle. His eyes were strained by the glow of passing headlights.

Dawnay was relieved when he reached the semicircle of an elegant Georgian country house with two magnificent arcades arching from either wing. A butler came out to greet him.

He was ushered into a magnificent drawing room, and Grantley came forward to welcome him. He was alone. Lady Grantley had died two years before. 'Splendid to see you, old boy. Splendid to see you,' he said. 'You're lucky to come in a week when we aren't holding a conference. Now we can have a long talk and a bite to eat. But first, what'll you have to drink?'

Dawnay had to respect the man's nerve. A blackmailer treating his victim like an honoured guest. Dawnay accepted the drink and stayed on his feet, admiring the pictures that graced the elegant drawing room. Grantley provided small talk with the easy practice of the professional diplomat. He prattled about this and that, carefully avoiding anything that touched on the controversial.

Dawnay had thought carefully on the way

up about how he was going to approach the subject. He said slowly, once the small talk had subsided. 'You know why I'm here, James?'

The former ambassador just looked at him. 'Go on.'

'It's about the al-Dawah business.'

'I didn't think it was a purely social call,' said Grantley, grimacing slightly. 'So that's what I assumed it must be about.'

'Why did you do it?' asked Dawnay, casually.

Grantley looked hard at him and started pacing the room. 'I don't know what you mean. And anyhow, it's all over. Do you really still care? I'm sure I thought it was all water under the bridge, something I'd forgotten. Willie, there's really no point in dredging these things up.' He was red in the face and clasping and unclasping his hands, and his eyes looked anxious and troubled.

'You dredged it up,' said Dawnay languidly, like a fisherman playing a line. 'It would have been forgotten but for you. What did you do it for?'

The ex-ambassador looked puzzled. Then he said quietly, 'I thought you were a rotten diplomat from the moment you joined us, and your behaviour now confirms it. You hadn't the first understanding of what diplomacy is about. It's about smoothing relations, not starting quarrels. It's about understanding, not finding contentious points to argue about. You never understood that. I set down what I honestly perceived to be the political situation in al-Dawah at the time. I couldn't invent events, couldn't foresee trouble where there was none. By the time the horror took place, by the time the British government might have acted, it was too late. That was why I advised them not to.'

'Why justify yourself now?' Dawnay asked without sympathy. He was glad Grantley was so nervous, so defensive. It gave him the advantage, and he intended to press it home. He looked at Grantley—his face still distinguished, the arch of the shoulders still impressive and poised. Yet Dawnay thought he could detect signs that his face was collapsing, that his strength was failing him. 'You were desperately wrong at the time. You thought there was nothing in the air. I knew just how much there was. I knew that Islamic militancy was the problem, while you censored my despatches and wrote back to the F.O that the army was slowly taking charge.

'I knew, and you suppressed my view, and the truth caught up with you. The only thing you did right was to order the evacuation; to get our people out in time before the National Liberation Front forces took over the capital, and the real savagery began. But look at what you left: a communist government at the heart of Arabia!'

There was a venomous and total bitterness in Grantley's face. He looked at Dawnay with hatred, his eyes narrowed. 'Did McQuarry tell you? Was he the one who sent you?'

Dawnay was thrown off balance. 'McQuarry. No. I haven't seen him in years—since al-Dawah, in fact.' Grantley looked relieved. 'No, I guessed it must be you,' Dawnay said. 'It has your style, your imprint.'

Grantley's hand was trembling. 'For God's sake, man. Don't blame me for all of it. I didn't bring it about.'

'There was someone else then?' Dawnay was astonished.

'The revolution would have happened anyway. It was inevitable in a country like that. Sooner or later. We couldn't have intervened successfully. A Western intervention would have been a bloody fiasco. I was right about that, at least. If you haven't seen McQuarry—what have you come for?' He paused. 'Can I fill your glass?' Dawnay nodded. Grantley got up, anxious to have something to do.

'I think you know what I've come for.' Dawnay looked across the room, at the splendidly restored Louis XIV furniture, the deep-piled yellow carpet, the extensive French windows giving onto a darkened lawn.

'Stop going around in circles.' Grantley was irritable, flustered. 'What is it you want?' he asked, sitting down. Dawnay placed himself in an armchair opposite.

'Why don't I put that question to you?'

'For God's sake, man!' he exclaimed. 'Just to be left in peace. I've suffered my judgment. I'm old. Can't I live my declining years without this—this aggravation, as my grandchildren would call it? I've lost a wife, isn't that enough?'

'You've suffered for two years, I've had twenty-two.'

His face sagged. 'Yes, I suppose so,' he said listlessly.

Dawnay drew himself up. Now was the time. 'I want a confession. I want to know why you did it. When you've said your piece, I'll judge what to do about it.' He put his hand in his pocket and pulled out a small dictating machine, borrowed from the office, which he placed in front of Grantley.

The old man's brow clouded and his face looked thunderous, a deep rich red colour. Dawnay thought he was going to explode. 'Why,' Grantley said, 'are you doing this to me?'

'You, of all people, have the gall to ask that?' Dawnay laughed dryly.

Grantley suddenly pulled himself forward. 'And if I tell you to get out of the house?'

Dawnay's hand moved to his other pocket. Trying to keep it from trembling, he drew out the revolver.

It looked an absurd object, completely out of keeping with its surroundings, with these two pillars of the establishment: a middle-aged publisher and an elderly ex-diplomat. Yet there had been no alternative.

It had taken Dawnay the best part of the afternoon to find the weapon in a trunk in a spare room: It was his father's old service revolver. Dawnay had cleaned and polished it, remembering dim lessons from national service days. There had always been the possibility that Grantley himself would be armed. Blackmailers knew the risks when they started.

He jumped visibly when Dawnay pointed the weapon. 'Have you gone mad?' he exclaimed.

'No, and please don't think of pushing the button on the arm of the chair to summon the staff,' Dawnay told him. 'I know how to use this. I was a good shot in my national service days, and I've had plenty of practice shooting pheasants since.' He was lying. he didn't even know whether the damn thing worked. It was pure bluff. Still, it had been necessary.

The ex-diplomat mopped his forehead with his hand. 'For God's sake, I'll tell you. But don't keep the damn thing pointed at me. So: I was working for the other side during my posting in al-Dawah. I had been recruited twenty-six years earlier, in my university days. I didn't think I was working against British interests: It seemed to me that for the poor bloody people of that place, life could only improve if a revolutionary government came to power, as has in fact been the case. I was determined to make sure no damn fool from the foreign office sent British soldiers to keep that corrupt bunch of so-and-sos in power.

'I succeeded: After al-Dawah, I never worked for the other side again. They made no further demands on me, and in any case I didn't care for them any more. There: Does that satisfy you? Have you heard enough?'

Dawnay was so astonished he could hardly control the expression on his face, even though he had to for fear of letting Grantley know he had delivered himself into Dawnay's hands. 'It was no more than I had assumed. Your obsession with censoring my despatches gave you away.' His throat was dry, his heart was pounding at having to keep up the pretence.

'You were always too clever for your own good, Dawnay,' the older man said blackly. 'Where has it got you?'

'While this is where treachery has got you,' Dawnay said bitterly. He cast his eyes around the magnificent room.

'Who are you doing this for—the newspapers?' Grantley asked. 'I'm sure you're aware that the security services found out fifteen years ago at the time Burke fled the country. I told them everything then, in exchange for a guarantee of immunity. What do you require to buy your silence? Or is this just some damn form of revenge for the way I behaved to you all those years ago?'

'It's no more than tit for tat for what you've done,' Dawnay said. The irony of it all was sinking home. 'You stunted my life. You're a shit. They don't come lower than that.'

'Except—' he controlled himself.

'Except what?' Dawnay rapped out.

'For men who murder their wives.' He said it with a hint of smugness.

Dawnay rose to his feet, clutching the revolver. He pointed to his briefcase which was on the table between then. 'Pick that up,' he said. Grantley did so slowly, looking always at the gun. 'Open it, and take out the typescript on top. I'm sure you'll recognise it,' Dawnay added dryly. He said nothing. 'Now turn to page 126: the last but one. Read from the beginning of the second paragraph.' Dawnay had brought the gun over to where Grantley sat. He put it against his forehead. The ex-ambassador was sweating profusely, striving to retain his calm, his hands trembling as he found the place. 'Read it,' Dawnay said, with a trace of hysteria in his voice. He read, in as controlled a voice as he could muster.

FIVE

When all hope ends, one questions the point of life itself. I did so, as I lay in that broad, half-filled bed, waiting, waiting, not knowing for what. I tried to find security, as I had as a child, in little things. I thought of how safe and snug I felt tucked up safely in bed, while the horror raged outside. I enjoyed the feel of the sheet, and its soft caress, placing the top of it against my lip as I had when a child. I looked at the furniture, looming large and reassuring in the dark. I thought: 'It isn't the end of the world that you have left me.' I still had family and some friends who would remember me in England. I would go back, start again, find someone new, if I had the energy; I could rebuild the illusion that there was good in men.

The moments of hope, of reassurance, were interrupted by terrible moments, when I felt tired and I knew too much. I knew what the world had to offer, and it was nothing. We lived our lives, and they were lives of suffering to be endured which would lead us, hopefully, to an early grave. Every person had to struggle in life and the struggle was pitiless, because it was no more than one man and one woman in competition against one another, in competition to survive, and when they died they would be replaced by others they had borne into the world to struggle, and the struggle would go on, unceasingly.

There had never been any point in it, any of it, in all the competition on the diplomatic circuits and the competition between nations, and the competition between me and Willie. I was wise, too wise, and I understood the pointlessness of it all. I knew how the world worked, what motivated man, and the terrible reality was that nothing did: that people competed for the sake of it, and that it didn't matter. Better never to have been born than to understand that. And I wished I hadn't been born, or that I had been born without insight or wisdom. Willie's behaviour faded into insignificance compared with those terrible thoughts. I pitied him: He was just one of the competitors, and so was I.

I wanted death desperately, at that moment. Death would be relief, escape, merciful, pure, peace after the struggle. And then something in me told me to keep fighting, that death was the cowardly way out, and my logic sought to convince me that I was feeling this way only because of my bitter despair and that one day I would regain my happiness and my peaceful, outgoing nature. Then I would find solace in the little things again, in the feel of the sheet.

I could not sleep. I went to the window and I gazed out at the square, which was peaceful. Bright fires lit the night and silhouetted the crazy buildings in the distant parts of the city and a constant ululating could be heard, interspersed with furious, excited cries. The rioting was continuing. And I felt alone, alone in that strange land, abandoned by my husband as the horror went on. And I wanted to go out into the streets, to expose myself to the danger, to meet fear, to end it all.

Then my mind told me that I must fight, that I was being overcome, that I had been happy once and could be happy again, although it seemed impossible. And then I heard noises in the room above, and they reminded me of my misery. I wanted death, and it came to me, more quickly than I could have expected.

It didn't happen as you told the ambassador and commission of enquiry. You lied to them. We had always slept together until that night. And I know why you lied. You told them that you had a sexual problem, that you couldn't sleep with me because you were repelled by the thought of lying alongside another person's body. That's what you told them: a typically self-denigrating lie, which was all the easier for others to believe. Hardly any other man would admit to such a thing, even to absolve himself from guilt. But you were cynical, you would admit it because other people's opinions of yourself never counted for much—so long, that is, as they accepted that you were exceptional.

You told the commission of enquiry that they came in from the window, from the square, and the windows were shattered to prove the point, even though no one ever got into the old city to find out one way or another.

That was a lie too. They came in through the door—how well I remember the vivid streak of light from the hallway as it opened, the crazed eyes and lips drawn back across huge teeth, the sheen of the two of them as they saw me, hesitated a moment and then made for me. My blind terror drowned out the rest, and masked what they did to me. Only blessed, blessed oblivion rescued me as the knives plunged into my body and their cries rang like wild beasts into my consciousness. Then it went out, like darkness being extinguished.

Dawnay and Grantley were both bathed in sweat, as though they had performed a sexual act together. Dawnay hadn't noticed the quaver in the old man's voice, throughout the reading; he had been plunged back into that terrible night, and felt as though he had gone through the ordeal again himself.

Grantley's tone was very calm, although with an edge. It caught Dawnay after the long pause when he had finished. He said, 'I say, could you stop holding that damn thing to my cheek. It makes me nervous and it's terribly cold.' A little absently Dawnay took the gun from his cheek.

He kept him covered, in a loose sort of way, as he went back to his seat. Grantley didn't look in any shape to move himself. His face was set and taut with anxiety.

Dawnay felt drained of emotion. He looked at him listlessly, with resignation. But he knew what he had to do, although without real hatred. The inevitable had to happen. He said quietly: 'Why?'

Grantley replied just as quietly: 'How can I make you believe it wasn't me? I know now why you have to believe it was. But you know I had no motive.' He was speaking in measured tones, as to a child.

'That's what I want to find out before I kill you, the motive. It couldn't have been money, you're not the type that wants—more than you have already. I suppose it's a sort of retribution for your treachery, for the self-hatred induced by your treachery. Or a hatred of me that has grown obsessional.'

'Good God, man!' Grantley was close to tears, pleading. 'I hadn't given you a thought in years! Write a whole bloody book like that just to make your life uncomfortable—it doesn't make sense—' And then he stopped, and Dawnay could see that a thought had struck him and hope had flooded into his eyes. 'I've got it,' he exclaimed.

'What?' Dawnay asked, startled.

'The proof that'll convince you I didn't write it. God help you thereafter,' he added, an expression of sorrow and pain crossing his brow. 'Do you remember,' he asked slowly, 'our meeting the afternoon after her death, after you two had returned on foot, just before the evacuation began?'

'How can I forget it? We left poor Jill where she lay, because I couldn't bear to touch her. We had no time to bury her. It took four hours of scouting backwards and forwards down alleyways, trying to skirt the main crowd, before we got through. Luckily no troops had been posted to guard the embassy—' Dawnay was aware that he was rambling.

Grantley caught him up sharply, just as he used to. 'Yes, well. You told me the truth then—that you had always slept together, but that you had been sleeping with that damn journalist that night, and that they got in through the interior of the house, not the window. And *I told you to lie*, to cover up. I told you to say you never slept with your wife, and that the killers

217

had got in through the window. Dammit man, don't you remember? I thought you had suffered enough! You were shot to pieces at the time.'

'I remember,' Dawnay said weakly, because he knew what it meant.

'Well, I wouldn't have written a damn fool book like that, with that mistake about me. I tried to cover up, to protect you. Not because I didn't think you were a damn fool and criminally responsible—' (he checked himself—after all Dawnay still had a gun)—'for her death, but because I believe in protecting my people. I believe in loyalty to those who serve me. A square, old-fashioned view, I'll admit. Don't you see, though, that it couldn't have been me?' He asked desperately, angrily.

'But there isn't anyone else,' Dawnay shouted, as desperately.

'Yes there is,' he replied too quickly and quietly. He knew, and as their troubled eyes met, Dawnay understood what he was thinking, and he didn't want him to say it, because that would be most terrible of all.

Dawnay moved to go. He tried to get out before Grantley said it. He seemed to read Dawnay's thoughts. 'Thank God you've ended that nonsense.' He rose to his feet and came slowly towards Dawnay. He looked down. He picked up the tape recorder and pulled out the tape. 'I'll have that, if I may. I'm not going to call the police, but I suggest you leave.'

Dawnay rose mechanically and allowed Grantley to steer him across the room, through the deserted great hall, out of the front door and towards where his car was parked in the silent courtyard embraced by the house.

Grantley leaned towards Dawnay. 'To live with yourself, that is hardest of all. My God, how we've both suffered.' Dawnay drove off without a word.

SIX

When Dawnay reached London the house was empty, to his relief. He didn't want to talk to Sarah, or to anyone. He went straight upstairs, to the attic room at the top of the house which he used as his study. His mind was racing with wild, terrible thoughts. He placed the typescript on the table, then strode up and down, up and down, like a man possessed, trying to think it all out trying to find the alternative explanation. He could find none.

He looked out of the attic window where it overlooked the street, where a few cars hurried past, not caring, not interested in him. He found that oddly comforting: The whole world, at least, was not obsessed with his problem, which had become the whole world to him. He gazed at the tidy, orderly room, with its hint of bohemianness, of the writer's craft, in its cleared desk and its minor works by minor artists, the new, clean, wooden furniture and the metallic spotlight lamps. He had a kettle in one corner. He made himself a cup of coffee, but he didn't need that to keep his overworked brain stimulated.

The thoughts came crowding in, like homing pigeons that obstinately refused to fly away. He thought of those four men who had come back to haunt him: How much of a ghost from the past he must have seemed to them! Four men whose pointless existence was exceeded only by their determination to abide by the hypocrisy that there was point in it, and his determination to find one. Hugo

Hennessy, the homosexual who had found happiness in a wife and children, or thought he had. Did he deceive himself that he had escaped his past, as Dawnay had failed to escape his? And if he had, where had all the diplomatic life, all his cocktail parties, all his success as a conversationalist got him? What had been the point of it all? Every cocktail party conversation was a memory that lasted only fifteen minutes, every diplomatic posting lingered in the mind only three months into the next one. He had staggered through life, jumping from one stepping stone to another to save himself from getting bored, merely to lead another life of futility. Hennessy was more to be pitied than Dawnay was, because he had condemned children to existence.

And then there was poor old Pugh. At least Pugh hadn't Hennessy's unbearable smugness, at least he knew he was living a lie. Dawnay could have sworn that the old boy fully understood that his lifeblood, every penny he had made, was being sucked out of him by his new wife and children; and yet he didn't mind. He would mind if he ran out of money and she decided to throw him over. Poor old Pugh, who had been the social lion of al-Dawah, the man who Dawnay, in his naiveté, had looked up to, one of the smart couple who cuckolded each other with impunity and enjoyed it. Yet Daphne, behind that worldly-wise, jolly facade, had been desperately unhappy, while Pugh himself had in the end lost her and been driven to a poor second best. Dawnay had come to dislike Hennessy. For Pugh, though, he felt only pity. Back here, in London, such overbearing colonial types were the butt of jokes in his publishing circle. It seemed impossible that they even continued to exist.

And then the unexpected: Quennell, the gauche provincial, the embassy bore, was ending his professional life the most successful of them all, having perfectly adopted that slightly accented corporate facade which pretended you were in touch with the shop floor while your life in practice was that of a pen-pusher, like anyone else in management. Quennell would have enough money to live on in comfort for the rest of his life; he could probably even retire early, even bestow a lifetime of idleness upon his children. All the joys of a bourgeois life had been secured by painstaking, dull, dreary

Quennell. Blessed are the dull, for they shall inherit the earth. But if that was what life was about, Dawnay was glad to have missed out on it. Even a diplomatic life was to be preferred. He, Dawnay, had escaped into publishing—pen-pushing, yes, but among amusing creative people of wit, discernment, background and taste.

Oh God, he was fooling himself! He knew it: He was desperately envious of Quennell, of the way he had overcome his doubts and had succeeded, and even seemed to be happy. That was why he was trying to convince himself of the man's essential inferiority. The man had even hung onto his wife, while they had all in a sense lost theirs: Hennessy had given up the sexuality he enjoyed, Pugh's wife had run away, Grantley's had died, his own had been murdered...did chance, too, favour the cautious?

Then there was the ambassador. A lifetime spent in deceit and treachery, justifiable in his loneliness only to himself. He had climbed up the ladder of establishment success, he was respected, admired, lived in style, had embarked on a glorious retirement. But beneath it all there had been the uncertainty, the questioning of the system, the hankering after something better, that had led him to become a traitor. Perhaps it had just been a question of appeasing his conscience for the luxury in which he lived. Probably it was no more than that—he wanted to be at the pinnacle, yet could not bring himself to accept the tenets of a society that had a pinnacle. What a welter of contradictions and self-hatreds the man must have churning around inside him.

And what effrontery to have inflicted his treachery coldly upon those around him, to have helped stifle Dawnay's career in the cold-blooded knowledge that he, Grantley, was working for Britain's enemies. He had said at the end that he had suffered: from guilt, probably. That was the very least he could have suffered from. Dawnay hated him, with all his heart and all his mind; if the old man was driven to his death by guilt, it would be justified. For by the time you reach the former ambassador's age, life is not present experience but an accumulation of experiences, and his life was now indelibly scarred.

Guilt. Was that the worst thing of all, as Grantley had said? Dawnay didn't know. He was mercilessly hammered by it, of that he had no doubt. And yet he would be lying to himself if he didn't acknowledge that he had had many years of security guilt-free, not in a state of wild excitement as a publisher, but without too much remorse, too much boredom. He had had nothing to be guilty about, before the book had come. What now did he have to feel guilty about?

He gazed sightlessly down on the traffic speeding past from the upstairs window. It passed by, leaving him, not pausing an instant, not helping him. He felt the cool of the night from the open window. He cast his mind back, back to the night when he had felt a similar breeze mercifully chasing away the oppressive heat of the evening, flashing in as a naked blade to caress his back. The blade had come from under the door, into the spare bedroom, where he and Sarah had been making love like wild animals that night, over and over again. He remembered Sarah's body, so much younger then, unwrinkled, unsagging, without an ounce of spare flesh. That slender, sensuous figure yielding beneath him, the arms and legs writhing and reacting to his touch, the softness of her breasts against his hard chest pressed upon her, the sweet taste of her lips. How they had made love that night, crazily, like wild and hungry animals that had found each other at last and were devouring each other.

And then the breeze had come and had touched their bodies, and he had been glad, until unease set in. The breeze had come from outside. He felt her body stiffen underneath him, and he also heard the stealthy movement of men coming up the stairs. They had got in, downstairs. He had risen then; he picked up his dressing gown, which had been tossed on a corner of the chair, and donned it as quietly as he could. She had watched him, saying nothing. And when he had crept out onto the landing, he had encountered the figure with the gun levelled, the frightened wild eyes of the man ready to kill behind it. He had stopped short, conscious of his vulnerability. He was naked except for the robe he wore, watching the man. The man said nothing, just stood still.

Dawnay hadn't known what to do, assuming the silent man would kill him, assuming that death was coming anyway. Then he had heard the sobbing and he tensed. The man had raised his gun.

Moments later came the scream, the terrible scream that spelt the end of all hope, that had shaped his life and condemned him to a mental cell. He jumped, and the man with the gun suddenly moved away, down the stairs, still covering him. Dawnay hadn't dared to follow until he was out of sight and running and other footsteps had joined him.

He hesitated on the edge of the staircase, not daring to go down. He heard a gentle intake of breath behind him. Sarah stood there, in a hastily donned combination of trousers and white shirt. She went down and was out of sight a few minutes, as he watched dumbly. He heard the crash of breaking glass.

She was pale with shock when she returned and caught his gaze. 'It's over. It won't do you any good to see it,' she had said. He had thanked her with all his heart, because she had offered him an excuse for cowardice. As she came forward he had fallen weeping onto her bosom, his tears a ceaseless flow. She had been firm. She was the rock, the strong one. 'We must go. It isn't safe here.'

'Why didn't they kill us?' he blurted out.

'Who knows?' she said. 'But we must

get out.' And they had crept away, down the stairs, past the room where she lay, dead, unseen by him. And he had been afraid of the answer to the question.

Why didn't they kill us? That was the question: and Dawnay was afraid he knew. He was afraid, so afraid, that the answer was locked in a cabinet in his mind he had not dared to open. The truth had been erased all those years ago, because it was too unacceptable for him to live with.

He had been responsible for her death. She would never have come back but for him, to that high-risk apartment in the middle of the old city, as the murdering raged outside. He had remained just to stay with the woman he loved, just to be by her side, not to fulfil his responsibilities for the embassy as he had pretended. He had failed in his duty to his country, to his embassy and to her. But for him she would still have been alive, he had no doubt of that.

They had of course covered up the fact that Sarah had been with him. She had arrived at the embassy after that escape through the streets earlier than he had, pretending to have stayed at another house.

But he knew that most of the embassy staff suspected that they had been together. He had betrayed his wife, then left her to die while he survived along with his girlfriend. That was how the world saw it. That was why he had left the diplomatic service. Of course it had been no more than a tragic accident. But he bore the guilt and the world blamed him.

That was the kind of guilt he could live with. Indeed, it was the kind he could overcome. He had found publishing a merciful respite after the diplomatic life. The quality of its social life was higher. He had become more aloof, more introverted. He was confined most of the time to his office and the tiny circle of people around it, and to his authors like a mini-patron. They were people who depended upon him, needed him, whom he cultivated and manipulated. They resented him sometimes, but never too seriously. He liked to believe that he had shaped them, helped to fashion their styles—that they were in some way the children he had never had. It was an easy, civilised environment, where the bitching went on mainly behind your back, never to your face.

The ghastly circuit of working cocktail

parties had ended: He was able now to see only those he wanted to. Above all, his sense of responsibility had eased. He had earned freedom. Of course, he had a responsibility to produce good books, a responsibility to his firm and above all to his authors. But he was not responsible for people's lives in the same way; and there was a cosy sense of security. Even on a back burner, he had enjoyed himself these twenty-one years. Guilt had made few demands on him.

Then the book had arrived. And it had been tearing at the cabinet in his mind, the secret thought, the fear, threatening to unlock a guilt he could not cope with. That was why he was sweating hot and cold, why he could not sleep, why his heart hammered so mercilessly, why his legs felt so weak. 'Why didn't they kill us too?' That was the unanswerable question. That was what it all boiled down to. And he knew the answer.

No, he didn't. He must erase the very idea from his mind. He was shaking now. He didn't know, he didn't know, he didn't know. He sat down on the armchair, and got up again, and made another cup of coffee, and paced backwards and forwards, thinking how small the room seemed. He turned out the light and paced up and down in the dark. The depression came to him in waves, leaving him overwhelmed by hopelessness at one moment, suddenly light-headed at another. He felt a little better now, on finishing the coffee. And then the thoughts came rushing back at him again, and he knew he must follow them to their conclusion.

The answer was that the intruders had not been religious zealots. Nor was a man with a gun likely to have been frightened by the sight of a half-naked man or woman. If they had been Islamic militants, they would have killed all the occupants of the apartment. The answer was that they had come to the house with a purpose. *You lied to them. We had always slept together until that night.* Exactly: So they had. The intruders had known where his bedroom was. And they had known he would not be there. There was only one answer to that.

There was a cabinet locked in his mind. The image persisted. He looked around the room at the little-used filing cabinet he had bought in a moment when he had intended to set up a proper study at home, but had played with for only a few weeks.

231

He rose, his legs hardly supporting him, and tried to open it. It was firmly locked. He went to the desk, where he knew the key was. He unlocked it and mechanically opened each of the three drawers in turn. He knew it would be concealed right at the back of the bottom drawer. It was a thin file, containing a few bills. He looked at the last one. It was made out to him, an invoice headed *Mark Robinson Literary Typing Service,* written in a neat hand, with a receipt stamped on it. It was dated January 21—nine days before. It was for typing an untitled work, sixty-seven pages long.

He had found the answer. He had suspected it before. Now he knew, and he knew it was the end. Guilt had him trapped. He was resigned and calm, now that he knew. He went to the bed and lay on it in the dark, his hands clasped behind his head. He lay there with his eyes open, thinking for what seemed like a long time, because he had to be professional in his life, to the last. He rose and walked to his desk and started typing a letter. When he had finished it, he addressed it with his usual meticulousness and neatness and put a stamp on it. The stamp was underpriced, which would delay its delivery. He went down the stairs, thanking God she wasn't there to see him. He went into the street, which was quiet by now; it was two thirty-eight in the morning. He put the letter in the box across the road, returned to his house and went upstairs to the attic room again.

He had a telephone in there; he dialled 999. A voice asked him which service he wanted. 'Police.' He was put through. 'I suggest you come to 83 Whiteley Street,' he said dryly and put down the receiver. Then he opened the drawer once more and took out the gun which he had never unloaded. His only fear was that the damn thing might not work, after years of disuse. It did, when he put it against the roof of his mouth and pulled the trigger.

SEVEN

I booked a hotel room. I wouldn't sleep in the house, although Dafydd called me a silly bugger. But I couldn't be seen with him, nor by anyone who knew who I was.

I didn't want to stay with anyone else, although my mother pleaded with me and my sister and brother offered. I preferred complete, absolute anonymity. The hotel was curiously reassuring. When I got bored of the room, I could go downstairs and into the bar where a whole lot of people I didn't know were talking and laughing with one another; and although I drank quietly in a corner, I somehow found them comforting. I was reassured by their noise. I didn't dare sleep with Dafydd, not yet, even at the hotel. I met him at lunchtime at a pub near his house which was frequented by Australians. We ran no risks there.

Everyone was terribly kind and helpful. Willie had had the common sense to call the police just before he shot himself, so I was spared the horror, for which I had steeled myself, of discovering a body a second time. I had had to view it only once to identify it formally at the morgue, and the experience was not as terrible as I had feared when I heard he had shot himself in the mouth. I had expected him to take an overdose or slit his wrists. Where had he got a gun from? And how did someone like Willie know how to use it?

But his face had been skilfully done up when I looked at him. His face was set, his eyes closed. There was a bandage around his mouth. He looked like a man asleep, who had been in a fight. His jaw was dark-coloured. Otherwise his face looked perfectly all right, although it was stiff and his colour was a very artificial pink. I didn't have to look at it all that long, just long enough to identify it.

I had long prepared myself for the questioning. The police, instead, were terribly gentle. They interrogated me as if they were dealing with a child. I said I was willing to answer their questions, and even grew impatient with their delicate touch, which slowed the process up. They didn't go very deep. They wanted to know if he had been depressed lately, drinking a lot, oversleeping, acting oddly? I told them yes, which was the truth. There was no doubt in their minds. They were just going through the motions.

I had to summon all my self-control for the funeral, though. All of Willie's publishing friends came. It was a ghastly occasion. It took place in bright sunshine. I couldn't wait for the box to be lowered into the ground. I was frightened one of his old diplomatic colleagues might come, but they didn't. Someone wrote a four-line obituary in the *Times*, which gave bare details and described him as one of the most gifted editors in London. All very low key, really. But I still felt I'd rather wait before seeing Dafydd. And I still didn't want to go back to the house.

Dafydd and I talked it over, quietly, reasonably. I had expected the trauma to be much greater, that we would both have been plunged into gloom. And yet it was exactly as we had hoped: a release. His overbearing presence was gone—how many years had I had to put up with it! When I had met Dafydd a ray of sunshine had been let into my life. Compared with Willie's dull, precise, predictable ways, his dry, ironic, catty humour, his cold intelligence, Dafydd was lively, young, his moods unpredictable, his views original and questing. And he was marvellous in bed, bringing to life a body deadened by the years of perfunctory if frequent sex Willie had given me.

Now Willie was dead, and I had identified his body, and a new life with Dafydd beckoned. I was not yet too old to have children.

The book had been my idea, but Dafydd had executed it perfectly. He was an inspired creative writer, who could write a passage in an hour which it would take someone else three days to finish. But it was never enough for Dafydd. He improved and polished, improved and polished, until he felt that every word, every preposition as well as noun or verb, spoke the character of the man he was writing about. His great strength was characterisation, and he had taken to the book as a major challenge. He thought himself into Jill's past, as I had known her, as Willie had remembered her to me in his long conversations about her, particularly in the months after her death. Dafydd captured exactly her passiveness, her air of injured innocence, the conviction that she was in the right and that no one stood for better values than herself—although everyone else tried far harder than herself, out of politeness, to get on with each other. She had been the snob, not those around her. Dafydd captured that.

Dafydd captured her moodiness, her fine aesthetic sensibilities, her dull common sense. He pulled in every detail I could recollect from the period, including the picnic by the river known only to me and the Pughs—every little thing, because I could remember al-Dawah as vividly as Willie could. The beauty of the work was not just in its grounding in fact and the extent to which it was written in her style; it was that it was written in her style as modified by his, his dry matter-of-fact analytical prose underpinning her emotionalism. When I had read the book the first time, I had marvelled. And I knew enough about Willie's sense of guilt to know it would kill him.

His guilt. Or I suppose you could call it his selfishness. It had ruined our relationship, if there ever was one. He had lied to me, not to Jill. He had really been in love with her, in some strange way. Perhaps it was her body, or perhaps the lingering, pale image, devoid of character blemish, that persisted in his mind long after her death. Or perhaps in the full flush of our first passion, of our lovemaking in al-Dawah, I hadn't realised what a dry old stick he was underneath. I had nursed him tenderly out of his despair, and then seen him become an old, passive man, gentle and ironic towards me, from whom passion and the love of life had been wrung dry. And I knew it was because he thought of her all the time. He blamed himself for her death, and half believed he had arranged it.

Why didn't they kill us too? He had asked the question so often in the weeks after her death. I knew the answer.

It had cost so very, very little. I had been given contacts by McQuarry among the fundamentalists. I had interviewed them, and they had been more than willing to talk for my articles. The poor people in the embassy had no inkling of what was happening, while I was writing it all up for *Time* magazine, for the simple reason that they had no contact with the other side. I found it delightfully easy to make contact and I knew well in advance that the uprising was imminent.

After one interview a fundamentalist party spokesman took me to visit a young fundamentalist squad leader, Abd al-Massoud, to witness the preparations he and his men were making for the uprising. They were eager, friendly, illiterate youths. At first, they were highly suspicious of me; but this changed when I told them I would write articles that would enlist support for their cause.

After the meeting I had a quiet word with Abd. I told him that a woman had profaned the Mosque of Qunrah, the most sacred in the old city, by entering with bare head and shoulders—the greatest insult of all. This woman had been a favourite of the Sultan. She lived in the old city. I explained where. I offered what was to him a considerable amount of money—some $100 in al-Dawah dollars, which he accepted gladly. It remained only to give him the signal.

There was a thrill about plotting the death of another person that was even greater than the risks of war journalism. It was, in a sense, the ultimate achievement, the ultimate taking of destiny into one's own hands; my whole life had been a struggle to break free of the mould cast for me in life, to do what I wanted. To deprive another of her destiny was the ultimate defiance of destiny.

She had to go, because she was in the way. I couldn't stand her from the moment I met her, a dull, intellectual provincial with typically bogus interests and self-discipline. She was totally dispensable to the world. Him I had always admired. I had admired him as a girl in my teens years before, when he had been in his mid-twenties and so marvellously self-sufficient and self-confident. Now he was more so, a rising diplomatic star, someone who had broken into the establishment world that was the envy of those on the outside, those who worked in professions like journalism and were excluded from the real world of decisions and influence. Or so it seemed to me.

Of course I admired the independence of jobs like journalism. But I resented its low status and the patronising contempt shown to me by those I interviewed. I longed to be on the other side, although I wouldn't admit it even to myself at the time. And he represented that; he had made it; he had broken through. We would settle down on the diplomatic circuit as the successful twosome that he and Jill had never been. I had never reckoned on the way the stuffy diplomatic corps would turn its back on us after what happened to Jill, nor on the way he would break down. It was, shall we say, an error of judgment.

Yet plotting her death had been a flight of fancy. I thought the moment for it had passed when she set off with Hennessy, and I moved in with Willie. There had been no earlier occasion when my assassins could have caught her on her own, without Willie being present. When she came back, though, that same afternoon, I knew that fate had delivered her into our hands, had wished her dead. The row with Willie could not have turned out more perfectly for me. When I returned from covering the rioting and he told me what had happened, I made an excuse that I had to get my camera and a few essential possessions from my apartment. I walked the few blocks to where Abd's men hid out. It was just a question of telling them where to come that night.

Willie knew nothing throughout. The great sophisticate was deceived with no difficulty at all. And I was free again, for the first time in my life.

By the sixth day after Willie's death, and the third after the funeral, Dafydd was impatient. Over a steak-and-kidney pie in the pub, he gripped me. 'For God's sake let's make it somewhere. I can't wait for it forever. There's nothing wrong with your sleeping with an old friend for comfort. They don't even have a whiff of a suspicion.'

I kissed him lightly. 'Just a few days' patience, and it'll all be alright. We've got a lifetime ahead of us. We can wait.'

He looked incredulous at my coolness. 'I suppose so. It's just so damn frustrating having gone through all that.' I was flattered by his keenness to sleep with me. My enduring fear was that, as I was twelve years older, his ardour for me might cool and he would in time be disgusted with my body. I longed to sleep with him. But I knew that we had to wait.

'When are you going back into the house?' he asked.

'I still can't—I can't even imagine sleeping there yet. He created that house, it's full of his personality. He was just like a ghost even in life. I couldn't bear thinking about that top room. Let's sell it quickly, as soon as decently possible.'

'But you can't stay forever in that damn hotel, it'll cost you a fortune,' he exclaimed irritably.

'Let's go on holiday, where no one knows me. And I'll move in with you when we get back.'

'If you really think we can live in my slum.'

'Better than a haunted house.'

Yet we went back to the house on Tuesday. Dafydd insisted on it. There was a pile of mail—almost all bills. I put them to one side. We looked in on the drawing room, which was oddly comfortable and familiar, cluttered with furniture: I had formed a picture in my mind of a house that would be frightening and unfriendly and unwelcoming, but it wasn't like that at all.

We went upstairs to the bedrooms. Everything was tidy, orderly, neat, just as it had been when Willie and I lived there. Dafydd put an arm around me. 'Alright?' he asked. 'Think you can make it upstairs?' I steeled myself, and went up the narrow flight, which creaked gently, as always. It took an effort of will to turn the handle of the upstairs door. But Dafydd was right behind me. I went in.

The low cheerful room looked exactly as I remembered it: the couch to one side which acted as a spare bed; the desk with its clean top and drawers; the filing cabinet; the lamp; the framed posters and arty prints; the slightly chintzy wallpaper. The window showing the cars going past. Nothing out of the ordinary. It had all been cleaned up: There was no sign of blood. And yet on that very desk...

Dafydd glanced at me, and there was a dangerous look in his eye. 'All right?' he asked with a smile. 'No ghosts? They don't exist. It's past. It's happened. It wasn't you, it was him. His guilt killed him. He killed her. Remember that, and you're okay.' He said it emphatically. I looked around dully. 'And now you've earned the right to live happily.' I glanced at him as he came towards me, where I stood. His smiling mouth descended upon my lips. His hands began to explore my back, crawling down it, massaging it slowly, until he reached my behind, which he kneaded gently. I could feel the surge of power between his legs, pressed up against me.

We stood there only a little while, and then he was ripping the clothes from me, faster than I could get them off. He didn't bother taking his shirt off—not even his trousers; he just pulled them down and pushed me onto the bed in a wild surge of animal passion. I surrendered myself and took him and I knew I had to live for just such experiences as that, knew that there was no point ever in looking back. When he had finished and he lay spent and uncaring and exhausted and satisfied, my eyes roamed around the room, and the ghost was gone. Willie was something from a remote past, and from being forty-two years old I was twenty-five and a new life beckoned with this strong, handsome, brilliant, successful young hunk of a man.

We lay together on the couch for a long time, happily. And then I said he must go, because he could not be seen leaving the house in the early hours. 'For God's sake, love,' he muttered. 'It was suicide. There was no other possible conclusion for the police to draw. They're not keeping an eye on the house.'

'You can't be too careful,' I told him. 'Not just now. Please. I'll be alright.' He left, and I fell into a deep sleep in that room, and was not troubled by dreams of any kind.

I awoke in good spirits the following morning. The room looked bright and cheerful. Light poured in through the windows. I dressed, went downstairs and rang him. A girl's voice answered. She said he wasn't awake, and she didn't want to break his sleep yet, that he'd got in late last night, but she'd tell him I'd called. I was a little thrown. I didn't know what to make of it, although it seemed obvious enough.

I made myself coffee and investigated the kitchen, where there were still eggs left over from the week before. The telephone rang as I was frying them. I took the pan off the stove and answered it. It was Dafydd, chirpy and cheerful as a bird. 'I imagine you slept alright? No bumps in the night?'

'I did. It sounds as though you did too,' I said dryly.

'Come on. You know I'm not the faithful type. I'm not giving everything up for you. You didn't want me to stay the night, although I wanted to; so I called up Liz. Don't be a ninny: you're the woman I'm involved with, the woman I want, but I didn't promise to be faithful. I couldn't promise to be faithful.'

'The same night you slept with me,' I said stuffily.

'I don't spend myself in one throw,' he exclaimed. 'Christ, having an argument about this is just plain stupid. If you want me to stop screwing around, let's set up together, which is what I've always wanted. Okay? Let's meet for lunch and talk it over.'

I wanted to slam the telephone down but I controlled myself. 'Alright,' I said. I went back to the eggs. They were hard, by the time I ate them.

I went into the hall and picked up the letters on the chest. I went into the drawing room, which was sunny but a little empty now there was no one to wish me good morning as he left for the office. I opened some of the envelopes, reeling at the size of the bills. Willie had always dealt with them himself; it was rather boring to know that I had responsibility for keeping the house up now. My hand froze on the fifth bill I came to.

It was headed *Mark Robinson Literary Typing Service*. It was a handmade invoice, exactly like the one sent for Willie. It read: 'To the cost of typing Chapter Seven...' There was no price, just the typed words, 'invoice to come.' I lay there a moment, a cold hand clutching at my heart and stomach; I was limp with astonishment.

At last I summoned the will to call Dafydd.

'Don't panic,' he said. 'Let's meet now. Away from the house. I'll get on to the damn agency meanwhile.'

When I met him, his usually carefree face was taut and drawn. 'Nothing. They say they never sent another bill. I couldn't pursue it, or it might arouse suspicions. They sounded perfectly innocent. I've used that agency for years. I've always trusted them.'

'But if it isn't them, who is it? Who could have known? That silly mistress of Willie's down at Oxford? But if Willie didn't know himself, how could he have told her? Who else is there?'

'They're after money, that's for sure,' said Dafydd. 'Otherwise they wouldn't have sent it in that form—as an invoice. Well, I vote we go on holiday and forget the whole thing. I'm damned if I'm going off on a tour, as Willie did, like a wet hen chasing up potential blackmailers.'

We went to a small farm that Dafydd had rented in the Dordogne. The place was dreamy: a pretty little house, tucked into the middle of wooded hill country straight out of Corot. The food in the local restaurants was delicious, the wines splendid and simple, the peace and tranquility marvellous; and yet my mind kept returning again and again to that bill, that proved someone knew. Someone had found out. The crime had been as perfect as the last one: The last one had been executed in the middle of a revolution by men no one would ever identify or find. This had been a murder committed by the victim himself, without his realising that he was a victim.

But someone knew. And to have just one person knowing was too much. The grim thought flickered through my mind, not once but again and again, that Dafydd was the only person apart from myself who knew: Could he be playing the same kind of trick on me as we had on Willie? But no, that would be too obvious—or had he counted on me reaching that conclusion too? I tried to conceal my suspicion of him, but he looked at me strangely now and again as though he feared I suspected something. Oh God, the trust was collapsing between us, and it led to unspoken thoughts—we who had always voiced all our thoughts to one another. It led to arguments during what should have been a second honeymoon.

When I got home again, to the house in Whiteley Street, I saw the letter at once, and my heart missed a beat. The envelope was in his handwriting. He was dead, but he had come back, just as she had come back to haunt him. I tore it open. It was quite short:

Darling:

I hope you'll forgive my little joke with the invoice. But there was a point to it. You see, there will be a Chapter Seven. You will not be satisfied with him, as you were not with me. And now that he has joined you in killing, you know you can't trust him. He's young, he'll want others; but you've got the money, and he's had the experience.

Why am I going to kill myself anyway? Because I trusted you, and one must trust someone. Without that there is no hope. I realise now what I did to Jill. I don't want life, now that I know there is no trust. You won't either, because you can't trust Dafydd as you trusted me. You trusted me because you, of all people, knew I didn't kill Jill.

Oh, and by the way you can tell

Dafydd I'd have rejected the book. Its central character was flawed. When I searched my mind, I found nothing hidden there. The reason I had feared to unlock it was not the possibility of my guilt, but your certain guilt.
All love, WILLIE

I could have cried with relief. The whole thing had been his attempt at post-mortem revenge. There was no threat from anyone living. Poor, stupid Willie: He was the one who had got his characters wrong. I was not one to be unnerved by a thing like that.

It's a grey day and it seems to me that life has become like that. Looking out of the window, it all seems two-dimensional—flat people against a flat background against a flat, pallid sky. I look back on my life, and it seems to be only wasted opportunities (I feel no regret for the killings, mind); and I look forward and there seems nothing to hope for. I have what I wanted: money of my own, a house, a lover. He makes love to me, that is, but he never seems so overwhelming, so besotted as he used to be, as though his energies are expended elsewhere. I think he's got another lover—I know he's got another lover—and I think he cares for her more than for me. She's younger, I suppose.

Since my depression began, I've been on a course of pills, but they don't seem to do much good. I take tranquillisers too, and other things. I'm tempted by the little bottle, but then I'd be playing into his hands—he'd get the house and the money, and he'd be able to set himself up with his little bit on the side. Spite is a powerful force.

You were right, Willie, I have come not to trust him. But you were wrong, too, because spite is just what keeps me alive....

The publishers hope that this book has given you enjoyable reading. Large Print Books are especially designed to be as easy to see and hold as possible. If you wish a complete list of our books, please ask at your local library or write directly to: Dales Large Print Books, Long Preston, North Yorkshire, BD23 4ND, England.

This Large Print Book for the Partially sighted, who cannot read normal print, is published under the auspices of

THE ULVERSCROFT FOUNDATION

THE ULVERSCROFT FOUNDATION

. . . we hope that you have enjoyed this Large Print Book. Please think for a moment about those people who have worse eyesight problems than you . . . and are unable to even read or enjoy Large Print, without great difficulty.

You can help them by sending a donation, large or small to:

**The Ulverscroft Foundation,
1, The Green, Bradgate Road,
Anstey, Leicestershire, LE7 7FU,
England.**
or request a copy of our brochure for more details.

The Foundation will use all your help to assist those people who are handicapped by various sight problems and need special attention.

Thank you very much for your help.